JON SHADOWS

KILLING SHADOWS

AIRSHIP 27 PRODUCTIONS

™

Killing Shadows
© 2021 Teel James Glenn

Published by Airship 27 Productions
www.airship27.com
www.airship27hangar.com

Interior illustrations © 2021 Tedd Lehman
Cover illustration © 2021 Rob Davis

Editor: Ron Fortier
Associate Editor: Gordon Dymowski
Production Designer: Rob Davis
Promotions Manager: Michael Vance

ISBN: 978-1-953589-03-3

Printed in the United States of America

10 9 8 7 6 5 4 3 2 1

JON SHADOWS
KILLING SHADOWS

TEEL JAMES GLENN

Dedication:

To Jaime Ramos who built a fire under me and stoked it
with friendship. Thanks, brother…

And to E.T. who continues to back me up and astound
me every day.

Chapter One
SHIP SHAPE

While the storm raged on the ocean outside, Yuri, the bald Russian with the limp made us all get into the shipping containers at gunpoint. There were sixty-six others jammed into the steel pod I was in, packed shoulder-to-shoulder like sardines in a can or perhaps more like corpses in a mass grave.

My cousin, Dae Hoon, (who I've called Sammo for years because he looks like a full-faced Chinese movie star with that name), was being herded into the second of nine other containers in the hold of the wildly rolling freighter. Sammo shot me that look of "WTF now?" that I had seen so many times before, but not quite in such dire circumstances.

I signed "stay cool" and let Yuri back me into the container at gunpoint. The steel door to the pod slammed shut and dulled the sound of the raging storm with a sudden and deathly finality that gave me a chill. I worried about Sammo; after all I was oldest and was supposed to look out for him, but truth be told, he was always there to cover my back when I got us in hot water.

My fellow prisoners began to murmur their fears around me in a Babel of languages—Tagalog, Cantonese, Burmese and Tai-Kadai. The absolute terror was very clear in their voices. "What is happening?" "Why are we being locked in?" "What are they doing?"

Unfortunately, I was pretty sure I knew exactly what the ship's crew was doing.

I had guessed something like this might happen from the minute the rising intensity of the storm drove the freighter onto the shoals off Cape May, New Jersey. It was pretty clear that the crew was preparing to dump the containers—with us in them—overboard into the raging sea to cover any signs of their criminality in smuggling in illegals.

It was a tactic the slavers of old had used when they were afraid of being caught 'with the goods' while plying the triangle trade route from Africa in the Atlantic. It was as cruel and heartless then as it was now, but with the history lesson for me coming a little too close to home.

I was in the corner near to the metal container door, crushed by the bodies of my fellow prisoners up against the joining of the corrugated walls of our prison. The stale human smell of the metal box, where we had often slept over the last weeks, was already rank and airless but now the scent of fear made it even more oppressive.

I had to work to fight my own natural panic at the fouling air and used martial arts calming breaths to focus on my situation and steady my hands. I then put an escape plan into effect I had prepared as a contingency; Mom taught me to always have a plan B ready.

My name is Jon Shadows. My father was born Anton Chadeaux but changed it legally to the *nom-de-guerre* Shadows, which the newspapers had given to him as a globe trotting do-gooder, long before I was born.

So, along with the 'new' family name, I sort of inherited the family business as I grew up. That business was helping the helpless and giving hope to the hopeless—at least that is the motto of the organization he founded, The Shadows Foundation for Justice.

Dad was of Scott-French descent and my mom, Korean-Japanese. Which made me an all-American mutt, but being a mixed blood is a mixed blessing and in this case directly led to me and my cousin being in those sealed shipping containers facing a watery grave.

On one hand my background often meant I was an outsider to more than one culture, on the other hand, when I wanted to I could blend fairly well in several. Like dad I was tall and a polyglot and though I had to often dye my prematurely-white hair dark for undercover jobs, my features allowed me to infiltrate many places. In this case, among the refugees being smuggled on the hundred-ton freighter The Lady of Onega, out of Dubai.

The ship was supposed to be carrying a cargo of straw hats and sandals from the Congo but had a far more lucrative and illegal cargo: human beings. They were mostly Chinese workers with some Myanmarian and Filipino workers that had made it to the Arab nation of Dubai to work on FIFA stadiums and other projects. Most of them had their visas run out or had never had any in the first place and so found their way into the shadow world of smugglers.

Most of my fellow 'passengers' couldn't or wouldn't go back to their country of origin, so they bought passage on the freighter—often with their very last penny—with the knowledge that there was a certainty of indentured servitude for many years to come. They had hope of a distant, happy future in the Shangri-la that was America.

Poor deluded saps.

Their magic carpet was taking them to a sordid tomorrow of sex slavery and factory or farm servitude and most would end up in ultimate destitution or death.

I, being my father's son, had been contracted by the Department of Homeland Security in the States to trace the pipeline from start to finish and get them the information they needed to plug up a pathway into the country for terrorists. Homeland are 'big picture' guys in this story but I tended not to be, and particularly in this case was more concerned with the poor souls in that hold. And, at that moment, very much so with my own butt.

And then there was my cousin Sammo. I was the elder by almost a decade so I was responsible for him—mom and my Aunt Suki, his mother, would never forgive me if I got him damaged. Not to mention I wouldn't forgive myself if I got myself killed, in fact, I'd never talk to me again.

I hugged the side of the container and listened hard. Beyond the sound of the storm and the commotion outside the pod I could hear the screams of other prisoners as they began to realize what was happening. Then there was the sound of a forklift as it moved one of the containers to the loading port, the increased sound of the storm as the port door was slid open and the horrified screams of the victims in the container as the forklift dumped them over the side into the roiling sea.

In keeping with the Marine Corps motto of 'improvise adapt and overcome' I had considered the possibility of being locked in a container, but not that it would be in so urgent a need of exit. Fortunately, I had a little something literally up my sleeve; a length of piano wire with a premade loop.

In the corner of the container were several small holes and a metal hatch that were used by port agents to check the packed containers without having to open the main doors.

I knew they would have to crack the hatch to let seawater in to drown us faster, so I waited by it in the cramped darkness. My fellow prisoners were in a complete state of terror, crying, screaming and beating on the sides of our prison. It was like being trapped in hell and hard not to catch the fear from them, yet I focused my mind on that little opening at the corner of the container. I did my best to block out the terror they projected.

When one of the sailors stepped up close to open the access hatch I slipped the wire out as quick as a snake and lassoed him around the throat. I dropped my full two hundred and thirty pounds to the floor to tighten the slipknot loop so that it cut into his neck. The wire went taut and I imagined it lifted the guy a foot and a half off the ground.

The sailor kicked and squealed but the wire loop dug so deeply into his flesh and did it so quickly that he had no chance to cry out for help.

I secured the wire to a screw at the bottom of the container and crouched down, waiting for what I knew had to happen next. At least I hoped it had to. Around me the Gehenna of noise continued in full fury.

The dying Russian sailor's struggles attracted several of his fellow seamen who came at a dead run, but I had pulled him up so close to the hatch and the wire was so deep into his flesh they couldn't cut it off him. Their only option to try to save their shipmate was to open the door again and come inside the pod to release the cable on the inside.

The cold equation of it was if I got our captors to open the door to the container I knew that some of the men and women packed inside would probably be killed, even possibly myself in that equation. It was a sure bet the only way the Russians could get in to free their man against the mass of prisoners who would rush out at them would be to use gunfire.

It was a massive gamble but if I didn't take it the surety of death in the briny deep was all we could look forward to.

Two men opened the container's metal doors swinging them wide in one swift movement as two more covered the interior with AK 74s against the inevitable rush of trapped refugees.

When the doors opened the Russians didn't wait for any rush, but just cut loose with a burst of automatic fire into the first line of prisoners.

It was not exactly as I had anticipated but I had figured they would fire from the hip at more-or-less chest height, killing the first row of prisoners. I had crouched down and scuttled out of the pod on all fours moving in a peculiar fingers and toes 'run' that my Uncle Kengi had taught me as a kid when I trained in ninpo with him in Iga Province in Japan. It appeared more animal than human and was the source of some of the strange myths about ninja practitioners in medieval Japan.

In any case, I came out under the deadly lead stream and barreled into one of the shooters at knee height, taking him down hard. I did a shoulder roll up the Russian's body as he hit the deck, smashing my heels into his eye sockets hard enough to crack his cheekbones and at the same time smashing his head against the steel deck.

I snatched the rifle from the moaning man and spun to fire at the second gunman before he could react to my unexpected attack. I blew off the top of his head then put a burst into the sailor I had landed on as well, just to make sure.

The two guys who'd opened the doors went for their sidearms but before they could draw down on me the survivors from the container swarmed out of the steel box and took them down.

The fallen Russians screamed in horrible agony as they were literally torn to pieces by the desperate refugees but I didn't spare them any sympathy.

I was already moving fast toward Sammo's container when three more armed sailors ran around it to deal with the ruckus I'd caused.

I snapped up the rifle and sprayed lead at them, dropping the first two.

The third drew his semi-auto long gun up to his shoulder to fire at me just as my rifle clicked on empty.

I winged the Kalaznikov at the rifleman and threw myself to my right in a dive roll.

My gun was not an aerodynamic thing and went cartwheeling end over end in a near miss but the sailor still instinctively flinched enough to spoil his first shot at me.

I popped to my feet and raced around the near corner of another container looking for some weapon to use against the rifleman but saw nothing on the bare hold's deck.

The armed sailor doubled back to around the pod and aimed at me, catching me dead to rights with nowhere to jump or hide. My past sped across my thoughts in a lightning flash in reverse order. Women I had dated, my failed marriage, my father on his deathbed lecturing me on doing right, my first real, mad love—Maria in college—and then jumped forward to my decision to take this undercover job.

I watched the Russian's finger tighten on the trigger while I calculated how slight my chances were to try to dodge the hail of lead to come. Suddenly the gunman dropped his AK and clutched at his neck, his eyes bulging.

The sailor convulsed once then dropped to the deck and lay still.

"Don't just stand there like a statue, cousin," Sammo called from the open access hatch of the container I was standing by. "Get me out of here."

I stepped over the fallen sailor to pick up his rifle and some spare magazines and noticed the improvised dart Sammo had used on him sticking out of the base of the sailor's skull.

"Thanks," Sammo said when he came out of his prison in the middle of the swarm of fellow refugees. He had a wide grin on his chubby face as if he was at an amusement park ride. He ran up to me, breathless.

"I couldn't figure out how to use that dart to get them to open the door till you came along, cousin," he said, clapping me on the shoulder.

"Nerve toxin?" I said as I handed him the pilfered rifle.

"Yep, blowfish," he smiled. "I kept it as a gel under a false toenail—just in case." He looked up at the catwalks that led into the hold where more armed men were pouring in.

"Company, Jon." He raised his rifle and let off a brief burst that took out two of the new arrivals.

"Coast Guard must have gotten wind of us when we struck the reef," I said as we ran to the next container to open the doors. "Or they would have tried to offload all of us by lifeboats to the shore to sell us instead of ditching everybody in the containers." Sammo snapped off another short burst at the catwalk as we began to take fire.

"Well, they sure as hell have to kill all of us now, cousin," he said. "They killed at least a hundred in those containers they already dumped."

"I know," I said. The armed men above us had retreated back out the hatches and were trying to figure where Sammo's shots came from.

We ran from container to container and undid the lock-bars so that the occupants had a chance to get out. Soon the pods were all opened and the prisoners racing around in panic, having figured out what the sailors were trying to do. Some of them had lost friends or loved ones in the containers already dumped and their anger and agony was palpable in the storage hold.

"We can't do anything down here except let these guys out into a killing field," I said as we crouched behind one container, occasionally snapping off shots up at the sailors on the catwalks. "If we are going to give them any sort of chance we have to get to the radio room or bridge."

"So?" He gave me the same grin he had the time we broke into his high school in Iga Prefecture the night before he was due to take an important test. We almost got caught on the way out but they never tricked to us having changed the seating chart so he could sit next to a girl he had a crush on.

"Let's split," I said. "I'll go for whichever I can reach, you keep them guessing down here and try to keep some of these folks alive." I started to move but he halted his firing to hold out the piece of rubber tubing he'd used as an improvised blowgun.

"One dart left," he said with a chubby smile. "You can borrow the tube; don't say I never lent you anything."

"Thanks, Cuz." I said and raced off toward the back of the hold having to push my way through the terrified mob of refugees. "See you on the other side!" I called back.

I knew the layout of the ship from charts and had been on similar ships of the same tonnage, but the corridors were dark and the ship though grounded was still rocking as the storm-wind driven waves battered at it.

My bare feet gave me traction but I still careened off the bulkhead walls like a flesh pinball.

The sound of sporadic gunfire faded as I got deeper into the ship, moving by feel through the maze of companionways I hoped would lead me up to a way to put out a distress call.

I ran into the first sailor five minutes into the maze of corridors. He wasn't armed and was stunned to see my ragged form outside of the secured hold; I was, after all, just a slant-eyed piece of cargo that would bring him a bonus at the end of the voyage and something he never expected to see in the 'human' part of the ship. The sailor stood frozen at the junction of two corridors for a split second then opened his mouth to yell.

I had no compunction about springing forward then and launching a *shuto* blow the base of his neck, snapping his spine at the medulla oblongata to kill him. I was not human to him and it meant one less enemy onboard.

I was up on the superstructure of the ship by now and knew I'd be encountering more crewmen. Although I would have loved to save the UN court the trouble of trying them on slavery charges by doing them all myself, I didn't have the time to waste to hunt any of them. Instead I grabbed a rain slicker from a storage locker, jammed my size thirteen feet into size ten rubber boots and pulled a rain cap on to complete my crewman 'disguise.'

I only knew approximately where the radio room was but the bridge was a clear target so I headed for that; from there I knew I'd be able to get to the radio room in a jiffy. I had to get a wireless call out to the Coast Guard and let them know what the situation was on the ship.

I made it to the stairs that led up to the bridge. There was a bored look-ing guard at the foot of the companionway and he was armed with a pistol in a belt holster.

I approached with my back straight to show off my full six foot four but my head down a bit to shadow my non-Russian eyes. The guard didn't even imagine I could be Eurasian until I showed him what a spear hand to the throat looked like.

I liberated his pistol from his fallen body, kicked off the restricting rubber boots I'd worn and went up the stairs as fast as I could.

The scene in the bridge told me they knew about the insurrection in the hold; Yuri was arguing with a bearded figure that had to be the captain while a helmsman wrestled with the wheel, likely trying to gun the engines to back the tub off the shoal.

Beyond the three men I could see a mate with binoculars scanning the grey, rainy horizon where there were the vague shapes of what had to be two Coast Guard ships approaching. That made getting out a radio message even more urgent to have them aware of the murders in the hold.

When I entered Yuri had his back to me but I saw the eyes of the Captain go wide. The bald-headed gunman saw the officer's reaction and started to turn.

"*Nyet!*" I called out. "Stay where you are." My order didn't stop him from inching his head around to give me a sidelong glance. If looks could kill I'd have died right there.

"That's right, Yuri," I said in English (Russian is not one of the languages I'm fluent in). "It's me." He had been a cruel jailer for all of us in the last two weeks and twice I had subtly interceded when he was making advances on one of the women. I hadn't been able to intervene every time or I wouldn't have made it this far alive. That fact added fuel to my anger at him.

The guy with the binoculars thought he was being slick by letting one hand slowly snake into his jacket to go for a gun. Dad would have probably warned him or shot him in the shoulder, but in situations like I was in at the moment I take after Mom; I dropped him with a quick shot to the head. I didn't need him alive like I needed the captain.

"Get on the intercom, captain and tell your men to lay down their arms." I ordered. "Now!"

When the bearded officer just stared at me I lowered the barrel of the pistol very deliberately. "Do it or I will shoot you in the left knee. I only need you to talk. I don't care if you ever walk again, or if you ever have the capability to breed for that matter. Get me?"

The captain stared at me a moment longer, his eyes flicking to Yuri's then he reached for the intercom mike by the helmsman's right hand.

That was when I made a big mistake, I let my eyes follow the officer's hand for a split second. In that moment Yuri spun and fired his AK from the hip.

His shot went wide, chipping paint off the wall to my right and I fired back but my aim was spoiled by my own dodge. Yuri spun and my shot hit the Captain in the side.

Yuri drew a bead on me but it was his turn for his AK to have a stovepipe jam —a rare thing but the second time in ten minutes fate saved my hide where skill had failed me.

I raised my gun to fire again but the ship lurched as it settled on the reef and again my shot went wild.

I didn't try a third shot, fearing I'd hit the captain again, so I launched myself into the Russian thug before he could clear the jam. I shoulder blocked him away from the now sagging officer and we both hit the ground in a tangle.

I'll say this for him, Yuri knew how to rumble. He dropped a mean elbow on me as I hit him in the breadbasket but I caught it on my hunched shoulder instead of my temple.

At the same time I hit him in the floating ribs with the pistol functioning as ad hoc brass knuckles but could not get it positioned to shoot him.

The Russian thug grunted in pain but didn't go down. He was tough as they come. He brought up his knee hard into my chest and got the strap of the AK around my neck when I shifted to avoid a second knee strike to my face. When he hit me I almost lost the pistol as I involuntarily jerked from the impact and blood started to spout out of my nose.

Before I could disengage Yuri spun the AK to tighten the strap like a garrote on my throat and I found myself fighting for air.

I was still bent over so I sent a hard, fast ridge hand up into my strangler's family jewels.

Yuri grunted loudly in pain but didn't ease up on the strap.

I was starting to see red spots and heard a rushing wind sound in my ears that I knew meant I was right at the edge of blacking out so I pointed the gun at Yuri's left foot and fired point blank into his boot. If he lived the son of a bitch was gonna have a choice of legs to limp on!

Yuri screamed and stumbled back so that he ended up sitting on the floor of the bridge with blood spurting out of his boot but he took me with him, my neck still trussed in the carry strap.

The pistol got trapped between us with my right hand pressed against my own stomach.

The Russian kept both arms under his AK so the rifle sat in the crook of them and yanked up on the gun to tighten the strap further. I managed to get my left hand up to claw at Yuri's face and suddenly realized I had Sam's rubber tube in it.

My face was cheek into his chest and I tried to get my hand up to claw at his face but all I could do was shove one end of the tube up Yuri's nose. He sputtered but it didn't annoy him nearly as much as the strap was annoying me.

I managed to turn my head so that I was near the rubber tube. I had just enough breath left to blow weakly into the opening.

Yuri's gasped in reaction to the irritation of the tube and that did it; it drew the dart with the toxin on it far enough out of the tube to hit the tissues of his sinus passages.

In a moment the bald Russian stiffened beneath me and spasmed as he had a seizure. His body jumped and the strap tightened further on my neck.

I blacked out for a nano-second but when I came to was able to untangle myself from the strap.

I rolled over to point my pistol at the helmsman, who had not moved from the wheel, and the captain who was slumped over and bleeding at the helmsman's feet.

"Okay, captain, get on that mike and tell your crew to put down their guns—now! I will not ask again!" I managed to gasp out, my voice hoarse. I waved the gun at him and the crewman handed the intercom phone to his officer. "Tell them that the Coast Guard is coming so the only way to escape prison is to abandon ship in the lifeboats."

When the officer looked at me with defiance I added, "Do it or this ship will need a new captain."

I knew enough Russian to know he told them what I ordered, then had the crewman apply a pressure bandage to the captain's leg wound from the first aid kit off the bridge wall.

I made eye contact with the helmsman who was doing his best to do nothing to piss off the crazy Asian guy who had just killed his shipmates. "You stay right where you are, buddy," I said with a smile. "And keep doing exactly what you are doing."

The gunfire sounds tapered off and then there was the sound of the crew yelling to each other as they lowered the enclosed lifeboats. They were willing to take their chances making it to the mainland and getting lost in New Jersey rather than face U.S. justice or stay behind to fight the escaping refugees.

I got on the mike then and said, "Sammo, calm everyone down there and tell them that the Coast Guard is on their side. Then get up here to help me; oh, and I don't think you're going to want your blowgun back. I'll buy you a new one when we get home."

Chapter Two
OUT OF THE PAST

Sammo and I spent a long week in isolation doing a major debriefing, telling the story several times as we were traded up the food chain from the Coast Guard to Homeland Security and then finally a C.I.A. rep named Donaldson, who, it turns out, used to work with my father in counter-espionage in the old days. I was always running into people who he either worked for, with or against in the past. Sometimes it was not a pleasant experience.

When we were sprung my cousin went home to his upstate place and I made a quick stop at my New York apartment and an afternoon twelve-step meeting (one is always in recovery). By then I had let the dark dye wash completely out of my hair and it was its full-on premature white—as it had been since I was fourteen years old. I got a hair trim so I didn't look as much like a refugee and called Mom to let her know I was back. She reacted to my sudden reappearance with her usual gentle, loving tone and ordered me out to visit her, telling me to pick up some groceries and sundries on the way. She promised to make me my favorite Korean food: *bulgogi*. It was the closest she came to mawkish emotion, with the subtext 'welcome home.'

Mama-san (she hated me calling her that, which, of course, is why I did) still lived in the house where she and dad raised me on Palisade Avenue in Union City, New Jersey directly across from Manhattan.

The Shadows' home was on its own quarter acre and had a spectacular view of Manhattan as it was directly on the edge of the cliff.

It was an old, three-story Victorian house with its own yard that was stuck between an apartment building and another Victorian house that had been sub-divided into a beehive of apartments for Latino laborers.

Dad bought it in nineteen sixty when he and Mom decided their place in Gramercy Park in New York was too high-profile. She's been there on her own since dad passed away two decades ago.

It always felt like I was going back in time when I visited Mom, images of growing up there impinging on the present with every step. Still, I did a double take as I walked down Palisades Avenue late that afternoon—arms loaded with groceries and enjoying the 'normalcy' of it after my months away—at the moment I saw a figure across the street. The sight almost made my heart stop.

For a long moment I did nothing, blinking in the afternoon sunlight, staring across the street and sure I was seeing a memory or having a PTS flashback episode.

I guess every guy has that one woman who 'got away' from some missed chance, some word not spoken, or some word spoken in haste. A first love that burrowed into your soul like a worm.

Maria Martinelli was mine.

As I stood there looking at the woman across the street I told myself I really was just flashing back, that lots of women had a figure like hers, lots of women had long dark hair or dressed well like she used to. There was not a doubt she had Neapolitan blood with her dark hair, dusky skin and aquiline nose. But it couldn't be Maria; it was just my mind playing tricks after my recent brush with death or my homesickness, but when she looked up from her smart phone in my direction, I knew.

It *was* Maria.

She was older by almost two decades but it *was* her.

I hadn't had any contact with her for more than a decade, not since I'd joined the Corps and contacted her via email to apologize for how I'd acted back in college—part of the twelve-step, ya know?

Of course I had thought about her whenever I'd reflected on my life, even while in combat in Fallujah and Kandahar.

So when I saw Maria standing across from my boyhood home looking lost and stunned, I myself was almost as stunned as she looked.

After all the years I should have had little or no reaction to seeing her; I'd had many girlfriends, a failed marriage and a lot of therapy since Maria and I had been an item, but seeing her hit me in the gut like a fist.

I guess until that moment I didn't realize I was still carrying a torch for her. It didn't help that when she saw me her face lit up in a wide smile that was as radiant as she was in my memories.

She waved. I almost waved back but then remembered the groceries in my arms. Maria started across the boulevard toward me at a fast walk.

"Jon!" she called with an odd pleading tone to it that sent a chill up my spine.

I started to call back, as if to reassure her and myself that I really did recognize her but then I caught movement to the right out of the corner of my eye. I became conscious of the sound of an engine revving at the same time.

It was a late model dark SUV with tinted windows that roared out of a parking space up the block. It came on fast heading straight for Maria as if it was being aimed!

She saw it and froze like the proverbial deer in the headlights.

I dropped the food bags and raced out into the street shouting her name.

I dove, grabbing Maria at the waist and carrying her over the hood of a parked compact as the SUV smashed into the side of that compact in a swerve that would have hit her dead on but for me. The assassin's car continued on with a scrap of metal and sped off.

Maria and I both landed on some cardboard boxes luckily stacked for recycling which saved us both a bunch of bruises. Even so the fall was still enough to knock the wind out of both of us with me landing partly on top of her.

We lay panting for a few moments, and I had a sudden flashback to the last time—so long ago—when we had lain beside each other panting for a different reason and felt guilty for it. I worked to catch my breath and whispered, "Maria?"

She looked up at me with her bright blue eyes and said, breathlessly, "I knew I was right to come to you, Jon. I need your help!"

"It's that idiot driver that needs the help," I said between clenched teeth.

I pushed myself up on my arms and am ashamed to admit I was reluctant to break the body contact with her by moving completely off of her. It had been a while since I was that close to any woman. I didn't have anyone steady in my life for lots of reasons, one of them being the woman beneath me.

What with my having to go off on undercover assignments I figured it wasn't fair to anyone to promise any tomorrows. That fact and the fact that the woman beneath me was the icon of femininity that haunted me, my shadows' shadow, did nothing to make me any more comfortable with any woman.

The car was long gone by the time I managed to reluctantly climb off Maria and stand up.

"I'm…I'm sorry," I said, blushing. I felt like an awkward college kid again. "I didn't mean to hurt you. The car—"

She smiled a radiant smile that didn't seem a day older than when she had smiled it at me the last time. "It's okay, Jon," she said quietly. "You did save my life; besides you know I have a high pain threshold."

It was true. She once broke her ankle while we were hiking the Appalachian Trail and limped for half a day on it before telling me because she didn't want to ruin the trip—and another half day hiking out.

Still, I felt guilty doing a Rosie Grier on her and helped her to her feet.

"Let's get off the street," I said, leading her across Park Avenue to my mom's place. The groceries were now long forgotten.

I didn't have to introduce Maria to Mama-san. My diminutive mother, even at past eighty had a mind like a tactical computer and certainly recognized Maria. She had nursed me through my miserable time after Maria and I broke up, had in fact pulled be back from the brink of destruction and sent me off to the Corps to straighten me out.

Mom shot me a look of 'not again' as we entered the foyer of the house but I said nothing, knowing I'd get a lecture if I did.

I'd whined about being abandoned a lot after Maria and I broke up and I hit the bottle even harder than I had when we were dating. In fact I hit bottom after that. Rock bottom.

Back then Mom gave me a choice that was on point—move to Japan and live with her family to train in the old style up in the mountains or join the Marine Corps to get my act together.

I chose having Hajis shooting at me over Uncle Kengi beating on me three times a day to improve my character. Mom always said it was the coward's way out, but honored my choice. I think she was secretly proud of my choosing to serve the county over just a 'mere' self-improvement trip. I think dad would have been; he had been seconded to a Marine unit from the OSS for much of the Second World War.

I'd joined the Marine Corps and let Gunny Harrow and a bunch of other good men kick me up the evolutionary ladder to human.

Three hitches later I was ready for civilian life and to pick up my dad's business as a sort of private cop. Best damn thing I've ever done.

One never is a truly 'recovered' alcoholic, only recovering, but having a mission in life was the best thing for my type A-plus personality. I had been dry, day by day for a lot of years.

Anyway, Mama-san said nothing when I brought a disheveled Maria into the sitting room. Instead Mom played the perfect host and brought in tea for us.

Then Mom toddled out to leave us to talk, followed by her constant companion, Banzai, her little fluff ball of a dog. I knew my little grey-haired warden would be listening just outside the door waiting to judge me—once a ninja, always a ninja.

So there Maria and I sat in the living room in uncomfortable silence for a few minutes, sipping tea and just taking each other in. I felt like I was twenty again and it made me question so many of my decisions in the last twenty years; if I had progressed so much why was I feeling my palms sweat and had my stomach doing flip flops because she was two feet from me?

Maria kept almost making eye contact, her eyes so very blue, but when she did she then averted her eyes, shying away and staring into her tea.

We had gone very different ways after college; she finished her schooling and then went on to a pretty solid career in computer design, while I went on to some face time in the gutter. She had married well, or so it seemed, to a computer genius like herself, named William Carter.

"Jon," she started to speak twice, trying to explain herself before she pushed forward hurriedly to say, "I...uh...there was something about William back then, when he and I met," she said when she saw me looking at the ring on her finger, "that made him a natural leader of our little group of computer lovers like himself and me."

"I heard a bit about it," I said working hard to stare into my tea. "He created some sort of a new social networking site that went big." I forced a smile on my face and looked at her. "It seemed like you had a good life and you guys were a good match."

"I thought so once. And, *we* created it," she corrected me with a little bit

Maria and I sat in the living room in uncomfortable silence.

of bitterness. "The whole group of us became instant millionaires when Facebook went public and they bought our network "the Phool's Phorum' to keep it from becoming competition."

"I knew you were smart, lady," I said. "It's why I used to study with you for Trig class." That got a soft, nostalgic, smile out of her

"That kind of sudden elevation changes most people." Maria continued, looking at me over the rim of her teacup. "It did William." Her pretty features darkened. "He seemed to think it was all due to him and him alone, even though it was the six of us Phools who built the site."

"Fools?"

"Phirewall Phools is what we called ourselves back in school when we started as a club." She spelled it out and laughed with the memories. "Just a bunch of nerds who found each other and gamed and talked Dr. Who and Atlantis and stuff like that. It was all so innocent."

"It usually stays that way only until money is involved," I said with more of a cynical tone than I intended. "People can afford to be carefree when all they have is pie in the sky, but when they make any of their dreams real they start fighting over how to divide the pie."

"You don't always to have to be so damn right," she said with the same grin I remembered from college. "The others, well most of them, had never even had a buck before and either spent it badly or never really learned how to hold on to what they got. Not William; he parlayed his share of the money ten times over, became a billionaire fast. It was all he thought about night and day. Eventually ignoring even me." She said the last with real pain in her voice and I found myself thinking '*how could anyone ignore you?*'

"He'd really have to be obsessed to ignore you, Maria," I said out loud and smiled. I tried to not fall back into old patterns, but seeing her sitting across from me made that impossible.

"That's sweet," she said. "But you didn't see his eyes when he talked about his investments."

"He's not the first man who's lost sight of what is really important in life."

"You really have become a real gentleman, haven't you, Jon? A philosopher in your 'old age.'"

"My mom taught me well," I said, "She whupped me good if I wasn't the first, and surviving combat taught me the second."

"She did a good job," she said with a sly laugh. "But it wasn't just greed, Jon," she continued. "It was love…love for the power the money was bringing him. And it was more even than that, he…he came to love the very inflicting of pain."

"What do you mean?"

"He loved to turn the screws when he bought a company and forced out a lot of the personnel. He took particular delight in that." She scrunched up her face into an ugly expression I would not have thought possible. "He said it was for all those who had looked down on him and didn't hire him when he needed the work early in his career. All the doubters and nay-sayers."

"Pretty extreme way to get back at the bullies," I said trying to lighten the mood. It was a lame attempt that didn't work.

"But that is the point. He was the one who was the bully as a child. When I met him he was the wounded bird, you know, and hadn't really discovered his real talent yet."

"Real talent?" I wasn't sure where she was going with her rambling statements, but I'd learned long ago to let the client talk their way around to get to the hard stuff. And I was trying hard to think of her as a client and not an ex-love, trying to stay professional.

"He is smart, don't get me wrong. Although he wasn't up to the level of Mike or Julian or even me when it came to pure calculation and coding, he was truly brilliant when it came to seeing how it all worked together. He was able to see how all the pieces fit together, like a general in a battle being able to see where best to deploy his troops, find the weak points of the enemy positions."

"I knew a leatherneck like that," I said. "He wasn't good on paper but somehow, situationally he always made the right choice…an instinctive thing. My mom would have called it *muga mushin*…a fighting computer in his head. My dad would call it gut instinct."

"William had it," she said nodding vigorously. "It's how he saw all the things the rest of us were doing and pulled it together into the Phools Phorum, the site we sold. He was the one who got the best price for us, even if he was the one who made it go the furthest."

"I'm sorry, Maria," I was still working hard to keep it all on a professional level despite being hyper-aware of her perfume. "But I still don't see why you said outside you wanted my help. Help with what?"

"I'm done with him and his way of life, Jon. I want to divorce William," she said bluntly. "I want you to help me serve the papers."

I tried not to acknowledge the race in my pulse when she said that and keep it purely professional. "You have the money to hire a dozen process servers to hand him the divorce papers."

"First off, Jon, I trust you, not some stranger. I would not feel comfortable with someone I did not know and there are—other considerations. I had hoped you'd help me for friendship's sake."

"Of course I will. That is not the point, a simple server could do it without you having to even see your husband again."

"But I have to see him, that is the problem. I have to go to the annual gathering of the Phirewall Phools. It's a yearly meeting and it's required that each of us attend or we lose our share in the profits."

"Profits?"

"We sold the site but we all have interest in a stock portfolio William set up at the time of the sale. It was his way to get everyone to sell. Some wanted to keep hold of their discoveries and felt (I think now, rightfully so) that the site would have prospered beyond what he sold it for. So William found a way to let us have it both ways, so to speak. Nonetheless some of us were worried the old gang would drift apart so a provision was put in the contract that said we had to come together for an annual party unless there was some superseding medical reason."

"So you have to go anyway so—"

"Yes, so I decided now was the time to serve William. I have not seen him for almost a year. Though I can't imagine it will be much of a surprise to him. We haven't lived as man and wife for three years now. Not since my sister passed away. At the ceremony to cremate her he was so cold. We had a big fight..." She shivered from some memory. "And right afterward he had his accident."

"Accident?"

"The main reason I left William, beyond his new avarice and ignoring me...was his drinking."

That one hit me where it hurt. Hard. With my own history, the cold irony about what had happened to me after she left me, I almost laughed but restrained myself. Somehow it seemed lightning did strike twice. At least around her.

"It seemed that the more wealth William acquired," she continued, "the more people he hurt, the more he seemed to loathe himself. After we had our fight at my sister's cremation I told him it was completely over between us. It was all very public. The very next day he was in a drunken driving accident that left him changed. It made him even more unpleasant. That's when he bought The Lair in upstate NY and retreated there to conduct his 'research.' I tried to be a good wife...even if...even if other parts of our life were over. I tried to be supportive to him, but it got worse and worse, he became more and more unpleasant, until, finally, last year after the meeting I left him and we have lived completely apart."

She had become very stiff; her eyes glazed over as she saw the horror of her own past. She shuddered as if from a chill. "That's why I need you to come with me, Jon, as a sort of bodyguard. I can pass you off as an old friend honestly because William has heard me talk about you. That way he will not be suspicious and we can serve him the papers after the meeting is over. It will make it less awkward."

I looked into her eyes and could see real fear for the first time. "Why do you need a bodyguard?" But I think I knew what she would say before she said it and it gave me a chill to think it.

"I think that driver out there was in my husband's employ," she said with a desperation that tugged at my heart. "I think he wants to terrify me into either not coming to the meeting and losing my share...or...or...he really wants me dead!"

•••

"Are you out of your mind being involved with that girl again?" My little grey-haired mother was practically vibrating with annoyance as she gave me a piece of her mind. She had started out as Ondine Yagyu at five feet tall and though age had bowed her over a bit it had not diminished the output of her internal getting-steamed-engine.

She looked up and pointed her cane at me waving it like a red flag before a bull. I did my best to not think about the pneumatic dart in the cane (once a spy always a spy) that was pointed at my head. "She almost destroyed you once, Jonathan! And you are not all that much wiser than that now; I saw the look in your eyes."

We were in my father's old office that I often used when I worked out of the house or when I had a client who needed a place to lay low. There was a closed-circuit TV monitor showing Maria lying down fully clothed in an upstairs guest room, under the influence of a strong sedative. She was tossing and turning on the bed like a woman fighting a nightmare.

Banzai was running around chasing his tail while Mom spoke and then he saw the decorative ribbons she had hanging from her cane and started to jump at them.

"Mama-san," I said using the term I'd called her most of my life to annoy her with its political incorrectness. I knew it infuriated her and I was feeling a real need to lash out, probably because I knew she was right. "Maria is only now a client—"

"She is a menace! She is bad to your mental health," Mom spat. "She drove you into the bottle when she left you—"

"That was twenty years ago!"

"And I see that same cow eyes on you that you made at her then. It is not her problem, son, it is inside you. You were not centered. I see you falling out of balance again now." I had nothing to say to that as the two of us stood glaring at each other to the sound of Banzai snapping at the ribbons.

I had no way to repudiate her accusation or deny it. I was a little terrified that she was right; I felt feelings I had long thought dead and buried.

But I *was* a professional who had been asked in my professional capacity to help someone. At least I kept telling myself that, so I tried a different tack. "Dad had set up the Shadows Foundation to help people regardless of personal feelings. She asked for my help so how can I turn her down in good conscience?"

"By sending her to someone else!" Mom insisted. "There are many private security agencies who could take her case." She swatted the dog away to send him scurrying to a dog bed in the corner where he watched us and the ribbons with a wary eye. "And don't try to use your father against me; he often sent people to Synn or Clark Savage or any number of others when it made more sense."

"But she came to me," I shot back. "And one of the very last things dad said to me was, "Be there when you're needed; it's my only regret that I wasn't there for Hank.""

I saw a shadow pass across Mom's eyes at my low blow. She muttered, "*The Chinese girl*," under her breath.

My parents had, to say the least, a colorful history. He had been paralyzed in a plane crash and had been nursed back to health by monks in a hidden monastery in Northern Korea. When he recovered to a remarkable degree of physical skill dad had practiced *Sulsa-do,* an off-shoot of the ancient form of *Hwa Rang* who were the knights of Korea. It meant "The way of the Flowering Knights." It was created by a Buddhist monk Won Kwang Bopsa to train the elite of the noble class in the 13th century and with the skills he gave them they were able to repel Chinese invaders many times. Dad came out of that monastery a man with a mission—to help the helpless.

Mom had tried to kill dad when they first met, but it was all in the line of duty; she was a teenage *kuniochi*—a ninja assassin working for the Japanese government just prior to WWII and he was working against the Nipponese Empire in Manchuria as an agent of the League of Nations.

They'd apparently had other encounters during World War Two as enemies but always with 'something more' and during all that time dad had been 'keeping company' with a Chinese girl named Han Ku Lee, 'Hank,' who he actually met in New York but frequently went to China with.

I don't know how Hank died late in the war; neither of my parents would ever talk about it, but it affected Dad deeply. He apparently went a little crazy, if news reports are to be believed, as he had a reputation in the latter days of the war as 'The Shadow of Death,' for agents of the Rising Sun.

When Mom and he had met and finally worked together in postwar Japan the 'shadow' of Hank was always there, even long after they became a couple.

Yet I know he had loved Mom with all his heart and she him, deeply and with an intensity and level of trust I had never experienced in civilian life. The closest I'd come had been with the men and women I'd taken fire with in the Middle East. Never in my private life, not even in my brief marriage.

I immediately felt like a heel for throwing the ghost into the mix and said, "I am sorry if it upsets you, but I have to do this, *okasan*."

She took note of my use of an informal, but correct and non-inflammatory title for her and I saw her posture relax a bit.

"What is your next step?" she asked in a neutral voice and I could tell she was already calculating different possible scenarios and waiting to see what one I would select.

Not the least bit judgmental, my mom. Not at all.

"To keep her off the grid for the next week, in case that car was actually an attack on her life," I accepted her olive branch. "And do some investigation of her husband as deep background."

"Where?" I detected just a hint of 'not here!' in her tone.

"I thought I'd stash her at Sammo's," I replied. "He's set up to handle secure guests and even though he just got back home I know he is alone up there at present."

My little grey-haired general nodded approval. "*Hai*. He will be immune to her charms, and better to keep this sordidness in the family." She waved to Banzai who ran over and jumped up into her arms.

"Really, Mama-san? Are you that ashamed of my feelings for Maria?"

She gave me a look that could have frozen helium and just said, "I'll call Dae Hoon to explain things while you go out and shop again; Banzai needs his treats and you scattered the groceries all over the street with your clumsy rescue."

Chapter Three
THE OLD COUNTRY HOME

Walden, New York up in Orange County was as close to Andy's Mayberry as you were likely to get in the real world; a village just ninety minutes north of New York City with no building over three stories and an actual village center that looked like a back lot 'little America.'

It went back to the eighteenth century, beginning as a mill town along the Wallkill River. It had been a center for knife-making at one point, with the slang name of 'Knifetown,' which I think was the ironic reason that Sammo moved there.

Dae Hoon owned a blue-collar takeout Chinese restaurant in the middle of the village on Orange Avenue and a high-end Japanese Restaurant just outside town accessible to NY 208. He actually had a talent for management and made a good living with it, but, as is always the case with traditional Ninpo practitioners, it was all a cover.

We *ninjitsu* practioners are trained almost from birth to be like onions, that is with layers within layers. Or maybe those Russian nesting dolls. Bottom line is that in Ninpo you do not present your true face to many and always have a hold card and an escape hole.

Mind you, Ninpo is not the cartoon black pajama guys you see in the movies; it started out as the special forces/spies of the Samurai class, made up of disenfranchised farmers and low-level samurai in the Iga and Koga Prefectures. And while we were big on tradition the art has always been the cutting edge of sneaky technology and warfare so we were as much about guns and computers as we were about swords and knives. And we were all about multiple identities and escape routes.

Sammo had his identity as a successful restaurantuer, a lovely Victorian house on the outskirts of town on a dead-end street with two acres of woods, and a live-in boyfriend who had no idea who he really was. Outside of Walden my cousin was a top operative in the extensive network of security specialists that was our family.

"Hey, Cuz," Sammo greeeted me as I pulled up in front of his purple and red turreted home. He was on his knees in the front of the house pruning a rose bush. "What's up?"

He was looking healthier than the last time I'd seen him after the debriefings and I had to guess it was due to his boyfriend's cooking (among other things). They had been together two years and I knew Dae Hoon had to up his workout to compensate for Robert's gourmet meals. The cruelty of our job had been that Dae Hoon had just gotten home but Robert had to leave that day out of nearby Stewart Airport so they only had last night together. Still he looked happy.

I gave Sammo some hand signs that Maria couldn't see that told him that there was no immediate danger, but that I was there on a case. He returned surreptitious signs that we would talk privately later.

"Just thought we'd stop by for a visit," I said aloud. "This is Maria. Maria, this is my cousin Dae Hoon."

Sammo dusted his hands off and shook her hand. He was just barely taller than her though easily twice as wide.

"Nice to meet you, "he said with a full-on grin. "I'm ready for a break. Come on up to the porch for some lemonade." He set his pruning shears down and led us up to the wide veranda and indicated some wicker chairs.

"I'll grab the drinks and be right out." He smiled again and signed to me *"I'll do security sweep,"* then went inside.

"Is he really your cousin?" Maria asked.

I laughed. "Yes. Though I am sure there are times he wishes he wasn't; I seem to get him into lots of trouble." I sat back against the wicker chair with a deep sigh. I always felt more relaxed around Sammo. He was one of the few people in the world I knew I could absolutely trust. I knew he had a state-of-the-art security system for his little castle; motion detectors, cameras, the works. There were few places outside of my own home that I had more faith in as a refuge.

"And now you bring me and my trouble," she said with a dark tone.

"Stop that. You are not trouble, you are…my friend. I don't anticipate anything up here; this is about as far off the beaten path as it gets. But Dae Hoon has a good security system on this place and the advantage of great food without leaving the property. It will only be this week and I'll come back up in a day or so. Think of it as a bed and breakfast in the country and just try to relax."

I saw she was trying to relax, forcing a smile and I put my hand on hers across the little wicker table.

"Its okay, Maria. I promise; have I ever broken my promise to you?"

Before she could answer Sammo came back with a tray with a carafe of lemonade, some glasses and homemade cookies.

"Gluten free," he said as he poured drinks for us. "Robert made them yesterday. I'm sorry he isn't here but his mom is sick and he had to fly out of Stewart to Florida today."

"Yes, I was sorry to hear that last night, but that makes it a little more convenient, I hope," I said. "I was hoping you could put Maria up for a week on the QT."

"Sure, there's always guest room here. And it will be nice to have company. There is so much to do around the place since I was away for so long; Robert was fine at keeping track of the books for the restaurants, but he let my garden go to pot."

"I can be useful," Maria piped in, "I have a little bit of a green thumb, if I do say so myself."

"Great; you're caught now!" Sammo toasted her with a glass of the lemonade. "Consider it your rent; I have a whole hedge that needs replanting."

"That reminds me," I said to him, "*Okasan* wanted me to get a packet of rose seeds from you for her backyard garden; she said you also had some cucumbers and spinach for her *Bachan*."

"Yes, I have some fresh cut today I'll put in a bag for you to take back."

We sat and chatted about Mom's vain attempt to get a garden going in the back yard (perhaps the only thing she had ever failed at), of the weather and of nothing in particular for a bit, looking out from the porch to a lovely view of the river valley and sipping the drinks. The cookies were actually pretty good for healthy stuff.

We never mentioned our recent excursion or any 'business' stuff, not in front of a 'civilian' though I could tell Sammo was curious why I had brought her and what it was all about.

After a bit Maria excused herself to visit the john and Sammo and I could finally talk shop.

"Is this the same Maria from college?" he asked me with an accusing eyebrow.

"*Et tu, Brute*?" I said. He shrugged. He remembered my fall from grace and had been a confidant for much of what came after. I filled him in on Maria's return and what I knew so far.

"So, I'll consider it a yellow alert. I don't have to be out of here more than an hour or so a day to check on the restaurants; they pretty much run themselves and I can do most ordering and such from the computer here. I'll keep all the perimeter alarms on."

"It might be nothing, but—"

"Always plan for the worst," he finished.

"Yes, and remember her husband is a computer genius."

"All my security systems are isolated, so nobody can hack in and override them. I use a separate computer for my legitimate business stuff, you know that. Aunt Ondine pounded that encapsulation concept into my head."

"I know, I know." I put a hand on his arm. "Thanks, Sammo. I'll owe you on this." He laughed.

"I'll add it to the very extensive ledger!" Now it was my turn to laugh.

I tried to give him the stink eye for that but we both broke up and started laughing.

Maria found us both still laughing when she got back, but over an old story.

"I suppose it was a dirty joke?" she said.

"Only dirty in that Jon changed my aunt's suntan lotion with purple vegetable dye," Sammo said.

"Oh, come on," I argued. "I didn't realize it was permanent dye when I added it to the lotion from her herbal stores."

Sammo snickered. "Auntie Ondine looked like a Smurf for a week and Jon couldn't sit down for two."

"I was fourteen, for gosh sakes," I insisted, "I really didn't know."

"Your little mother whipped your butt?" Maria said, giggling.

"Only because dad didn't let her kill me. She was pretty ready to do it, but dad was laughing so hard he said it was worth the entertainment value to keep me around."

Sammo did his best to embarrass me with a couple of more family stories and then it was time for me to head out. I stood up.

"You feel like a workout while you're up here?" Sammo asked. "I just cleaned the dojo and after all this kneeling in the dirt I could use it to loosen up. On our 'recent trip' we didn't have a lot of mat time; one gets rusty."

I looked at Maria and saw that she was smiling at the thought of seeing me and Sammo sweating. "Could I watch?" she asked.

"I don't know if Jon could stand the shame of losing in front of a witness."

"I've got the time," I sneered. "I have to figure what my next move is in this case, and it will help me clear my head; with Robert away you'll need to work off steam."

He shot me a puckered look then arched an eyebrow at Maria and snickered.

His meaning was clear but I guess he wasn't half wrong.

"Let's go," I said. "We'll see who Maria gets to watch fall on their butt!"

Maria clapped like a little girl. "Oh, I love grudge matches!"

Chapter Four
RANDORI

Most of my life the martial arts training hall—a *dojo* in my mother's Japanese style or a *dojang* in my dad's Korean style—had been the sacred space where any problems I had were washed away in a tide of sweat and technique.

I'd helped Sammo build his dojo in a traditional style out back of his house over the course of three months; it was about the size of a garage, though longer, built on stilts with an oak floor and cherrywood uprights. We entered in the lower left with a *shomen* off to the right, and a *shinto* shrine with a fresh flower arrangement.

That was the *kamiza*, the "place of honor." On the wall was the kanban, the scroll that authorized Sammo to teach Iga the style of ninjitsu. As it was a personal *dojo* there were *no kun*, or *dojo* rules displayed at the *shomen* as well. Weapons and other training gear were along the back wall, including a couple of Mongolian-style short recurved bows that Sammo enjoyed shooting. He had even set up archery butts and targets at the far end of the building. He found shooting a couple of dozen arrows a day—as opposed to the hundreds our ancestors shot in training—was calming. He was a dead shot with it and had taught me.

When we entered there was a small space to remove shoes, as we never wore them on the fighting mats. and to change behind *shoji* screens. From there one stepped up onto the raised area of the *tatami* mats, woven from reeds, that were the only 'defense' against that oak floor when you were thrown.

"*Randori?*" Sammo asked while we changed behind the *shoji* screens. We wore simple white *gi*—heavy canvas jacket and short pants, with the jacket closed by sash-like cotton belts. Both of us wore white belts, even though we had several black belts but it didn't matter to either of us; we had nothing to show off.

"Sure," I agreed. *Randori* was free play in jujutsu, where we basically just chucked each other around. Roughhousing of our childhood days carried to the technical perfection of a martial art.

One of the major aspects of the dojo was *shibumi*, a term that roughly translates as "austere" or "without complications." *Shibumi* is to include just what is needed, in its simplest and most efficient form. Hence no flashy uniforms and no need to boast with belts or ranks. Certainly not between Sammo and me.

"Do I have to get bandages and liniment ready?" Maria teased as Sammo and I stretched and warmed up before we bowed onto the mat.

"Maybe for Jon," Sammo grinned. "I think he's been getting soft with Auntie Ondine's cooking."

"One meal since I've been back," I said. "Makes me even with you and Robert's calorie casseroles!"

We bowed to each other on the mat and I leapt forward to seize his *gi* then we 'played.'

For thirty minutes or so we tossed each other with vigor and ruthless skill, alternately grinning, yelping and occasionally cursing in four languages.

After I hit the deck from a particularly vigorous *osoto gari*—a large outer reaping throw—I saw Maria, who was seated on a bench near the door, lean in and wince.

"Sure I don't have to get the liniment for you?" she asked.

I stood, turned to bow to Sammo and quipped over my shoulder to her, "You really know how to hurt a guy!" Then I moved in to fake Sammo out with a grab and swept him hard to the mat.

"Okay," Sammo said. "I'll take that liniment, Miss Carter." I helped him up and we bowed out. We hugged and laughed.

"Good one," he said. "We both needed that after the time on the ship, Cuz."

"Yes, we did," I said, patting him on the back.

"Want to put on the kendo armor?" Sammo asked.

"Not today," I said. "By the time I get showered and back to the city I'll just about beat rush hour traffic. I want to get started on the investigation."

"I'll head to the house and hose myself down," Sammo said, and turned to Maria. "Your room is stocked with towels and stuff. I'll get lemonade ready for us before you head out." If it were just him and I we would have showered on the outside shower, but I didn't think Maria deserved that much of a free show.

Sammo bowed out of the mat and stepped down near Maria to slip on shoes. Then he headed out of the dojo to leave me and Maria alone.

"That was pretty impressive," she said. "You guys looked like you were really trying to hurt each other."

I toweled off some sweat and laughed. "Well, we weren't trying to hurt each other, but we don't pull technique when we train—we just don't always go in for the kill move."

"Isn't that dangerous?" she asked. I slipped on shoes, grabbed my clothes and we headed out of the *dojo* toward the house.

"Not as dangerous as not being prepared when we get into a real fight; train hard and fight easy," I quoted, "train easy and fight hard. There are few people I trust like Dae Hoon. And we were on a job together for some months without a chance to really workout. We needed to knock the rust off."

"I really didn't understand."

"What do you mean?"

"I knew you are considered a top tier professional at what you do. And I know you served in the Marines and all, but...but...somehow I never really thought about how serious it all is. How...dangerous what you do really is."

I shrugged. "One could get killed just as easily crossing the street."

She stuck out her tongue at me and blew a raspberry. "Don't make fun; what you do *is* dangerous."

"Yes, but I was almost literally born to it. I tried to turn my back on it for a time. I mean, who wants to go into the family business? My father was an almost impossible figure to live up to."

"But you did take up the mantle. When I asked around they said you are the guy to go to if there is no one else."

"To help the helpless, to give hope the hopeless," I quoted. "That was Dad's motto and his rules of engagement." I shrugged. "I guess in the end I am my father's son."

"*And my mother's*," I thought.

"I'm not hopeless anymore," she said. "Not since this morning."

Maria stood as well and for a moment I thought she would reach out to grab me, but she just smiled. "You need that shower. Better to get going before I'm overcome by your 'glow.' I am downwind of you."

"As you command. I'll be down in fifteen minutes." I let her in the back door and made sure to put the security system on.

"I...I don't know how to repay you." She stopped me for heading upstairs in a voice almost a whisper. "I...I feel for the first time in a while that it will all work out."

We stood very close and the scent of her perfume was strong. "Just listen to Dae Hoon when I'm gone and stay inside. I promise it will work out."

"Will it really work out this time?" she said. I was not sure exactly what 'this time' meant and I felt a little dizzy with the possible implications.

I swallowed hard. "Let's just get through this. That may just be enough."

"We both needed that..."

Chapter Five
THE CORPORATE SHUCK AND JIVE

My head was in a whirl when I drove back into the city as I tried to get my hormones out of the equation and 'be professional' in my thinking again.

I only knew the public William Carter that the newspapers and gossip rags talked about, and even then I had not really paid all that much attention. Partially, I think, because I didn't want to really torture myself with stories that included Maria.

My first stop then was the public library at Forty Second and Fifth Avenue where I used their computers to do a little background for the public stories. All about not leaving a trail myself with questions asked and all that.

All the main facts that Maria had told me about, his rise to corporate power as *wunderkind* and the certain ruthlessness he exercised in spreading his cyber empire.

The car accident three years ago was only mentioned obliquely and Maria and her relationship with Carter was not mentioned at all except as 'his spouse.' So much for women's visibility in the world.

I took myself to Korean food in little Korea while I pondered the next step and went home to make a phone call to an old buddy from a land-line.

"Hey, Myke," I said to my old service pal. He had been a Coast Guard Reserve chopper pilot who I met in Germany when I was with a joint intelligence task force. He had mustered out ahead of me and went back to his pre-service first love with was, oddly enough, securities trading. He said he found it exciting, which I found hilarious after knowing this guy had run a rescue copter and been under fire at that.

"Jon Shadows? How the hell are you?" He had a high-pitched voice that sounded like it came from somebody who weighed ninety-eight pounds wet. He, in fact, outweighed me by quite a bit.

"I'm good, Myke. But I was wondering if you were around for a sit down?" He laughed.

"Deep thoughts, eh? As it happens I have no dinner plans tonight if you are in town."

"Name the place and time."

"Smith and Wollenski's Steakhouse, six o'clock?"

"You got it, and, of course, on me."

"Of course," he laughed again in his squeaky voice. "So what do I have to cram on before we meet?"

"Anything on William Carter, the computer guy. And associates."

"Wow, you don't do small do you? Okay, gonna be a prime aged steak and Napoleon Brandy, so bring your Gold Card."

After he hung up I called the restaurant to put in the fix for a private room that night. I would be spending a pretty penny for my private talk with Myke, but knowledge is ammunition in my business so it was worth it.

Only my name got me in, as it was generally booked up weeks in advance; I knew the manager and had been to several high-profile events there with big spenders. Sometimes being the son of a legend had its benefits. Being famous would seem at odds with the whole 'I have many identities thing' but, in fact, makes melting into a crowd easier. No one actually thinks a famous person would be working as a cabbie or a prisoner in a local jail, or what have you. And being perceived as a nonspecific ethnicity allowed me to blend.

After I got off the phone with the steak house I took a deep breath, thought, *in for a penny* and put in a call to Joyce Adder at the CIA headquarters at Langley.

After the usual switchboard shuttling, even though it was a 'direct line,' Joyce picked up.

"Jonathan," she said with a cultured southern voice. "So good to hear from you. Is this a secure line?" Always SOP with people 'in the game.'

"I'm calling from home," I replied. "As secure as it can be without encryption—I have a green light on my end."

"Good enough. Thank you again for the Dubai deal. Donaldson said you did his folks a big favor; I know that was a long hard undercover. Your dad would have been proud."

She was not much older than me, but my father's legend preceded me with the Agency and I ran up against it often. At one point I resented it, but you can't change history so I just grinned and bore it.

"Thanks," I said.

"So what can I do for you?"

"I am just nosing around something and wondered if the Agency had any interest in it."

"What about?"

"William Carter. I have nothing direct but—"

"*The* William Carter, the tech billionaire?"

"That one."

"Well, I am sure we have a file, though I haven't had reason to open it."

"Anything you could send along would be appreciated; I've done a public record search but…"

"Looking for anything specific, Jon?"

"No," I said honestly, "At this point just background, but I figured going to the source is quicker than reading more old Wall Street Journals and Popular Mechanics." That got a laugh from her, so I knew she was in the middle of something big for a low joke to shake her day up.

"I'll talk to the records department and have them send along whatever they can, Jon."

"I appreciate it, Joyce. It may not turn out to be anything, as far as a case, but thanks."

"If there turns out to be anything that would interest us—"

"Of course; I'll tip you to anything that would be in your yard."

"If you get down this way, we have to do lunch in person."

"It's a date," I promised. "Soon."

She hung up and the green monitor light on the landline went out.

"So there," I said aloud to myself. "Things in motion; stay professional. Stay professional."

•••

Smith and Wollenski was a green and white icon on the corner of 49th and Third Avenue and had been since the glorious olden days of 1977. It had pretentions to evoke the actual olden days of the 1890s with both the exterior and interior design. It stood out, if only because it was the only two-story building on the block of highrises in an area where air rights alone were a fortune.

It was a pricy place but its reputation was not only based on location or décor; the menu was highlighted by beef that is dry-aged and butchered in-house in a box kept at a constant thirty-six degrees Fahrenheit. It took at least four weeks before it is considered ready to serve which meant they had to move a lot of steak to keep the place going. I'm told they have upwards of ten ton of beef aging at any one time. That is a lot of dead cows.

I met Myke Tower out front. He fit his name, a six foot, three hundred and fifty pound black man with a gentle smile and the biggest hands I have ever seen on a person. I could never figure how he fit himself into a cockpit but he was a pretty good chopper pilot with no doubt.

He enveloped my hand in his for a hearty shake and the two of us went in to see Joseph, the maitre-d'. He was solicitous and escorted us up to the Skylite room on the second floor and a private table at the back.

We exchanged mild pleasantries and small talk until after we put in our food orders and Myke got his first drink. I had ginger ale.

When we were finally alone waiting for the food he sat back and sighed. "William Carter; you don't go after the little fish, do you?"

"Is he so different from the regular run-of-the-mill billionaires?" I did my best to not let the fumes from his wine distract me; once a drunk always drunk, you know? Even with sixteen years sober, with only one slip, *not* drinking is a daily thing. Most days I can pull through, either with my own inner discipline or by getting to a meeting, but in moments of stress it is harder. And having Maria come back into my life qualified as major stress.

Stay professional.

"Anything but, pal," Myke said. "Oh, he has the usual jacket; bright in school, ran with a group called the Phirewall Phools and created a social platform and app that he was able to leverage into a major company. He then leapfrogged that into a multinational corporation with a ruthlessness that would make Genghis Khan blush."

He pulled out a folder and slid it across the table to me. Inside there was a small encyclopedia of magazine and newspaper articles on Carter's companies; some I had seen in my cursory examination but a lot I had not.

"Of course, those are just the companies he officially looted or caused to take a dirt nap," Myke continued while I perused the company list. "The rumors are not on paper."

"Such as?"

"That he was pumping black money into his operation to clean it."

"Russian mob?"

"No one knows, though if not Russian it was probably Asian, but from where specifically, hard to say." The waiter showed up then with the steak and all thoughts of anyone or anything else disappeared for a good forty minutes of a great meal.

Afterward, we both sat with loosened belts. Myke sat back with his huge paw making the wine glass look like a shot glass. He had red wine and I was all class with cranberry juice.

"I am afraid I haven't been much help."

"You pulled this all together faster than I could have and you do have the ear to the ground; the dinner was worth it."

"Well, I still feel a little guilty. Nothing here is not public knowledge.. except maybe..."

"Maybe?" I leaned in, because I knew that if he hesitated to say anything it meant that it was pure scuttlebutt. I've found that rumors and gossip were often more useful than the stuff that a journalist was allowed to print in magazine articles. Rumors were not afraid of libel laws.

"Well," he continued, "they mention his car accident about three or four years ago, but his companies seemed to ripple then"—he waved his hand in a flippant gesture—"stocks dropped quickly with reports he might die, then there was a big buy from…somewhere…and the companies stabilized quickly. He withdrew then, went full on Howard Hughes. Got all weird. But just even more ruthless with taking over and gutting companies."

"Three years?"

"The exact date is in there," he motioned at the folder, "but yeah. He and his wife had a couple of public dustups about that time too, even before the car accident. It made all the gossip rags."

"His wife, huh?"

"Yes," he responded and gave a satisfied burp and smiled. "A real looker, the kind of a woman who could drive a guy crazy."

"Yeah," I said with a sigh. "I'll bet."

Chapter Six
SHOP AND CHOP

After a bit more chit-chat with Myke we parted company and I went to my apartment across from Gramercy Park on Seventeenth Street. I put on some bluegrass music and sat down in the living room looking out of the wide windows. I could see directly across the private park at the building my dad had his headquarters in from the late thirties until he and Mom moved to Union City in the early sixties to raise me.

I always felt an odd sense of déjà vu when I looked across the little vest pocket park to the townhouse. I had heard all the stories as a boy as if they were fairy tales. Dad's grand adventures and swashbuckling in Manchuria and the Pacific Theatre during the war, when Mom tried to kill him three times when their paths crossed. During the occupation in Japan where Mom and Dad finally worked together, when he was seconded to Army Intelligence and she was working for the Emperor and the new government.

Those stories were part of the reason I pulled so hard off the straight and narrow. I suppose part of the reason I fell so hard to the 'dark side' was a rebellion against that legend.

I opened the envelope to read the jacket that Myke had given me on Carter. Aside from having to look at magazine pictures of Maria the package wasn't that hard. Myke had summed it up pretty solidly. The details were not all that enlightening, except that I recognized a name that was mentioned peripherally as being at a dinner with Carter. Shinobu Tsukasa.

His was a name I knew from Japan. He had been the highest-ranking member of the Yamaguchi-gumi yakuza gang some time ago.

"So, William," I said aloud, "could that be where the money came from to revitalize your company?"

I made a mental note to contact my relatives in Kobe to have them see what they could dig up, but I decided to wait till I had a hot bath and a nap, with that steak slowing me down. I suddenly felt tired. Very tired.

Looking at all the pictures of Maria with her husband had a much more unsettling affect on me than I could have imagined.

Stay professional.

I had no idea what a can of worms I had stirred up or what consequences they would have for me and my family, starting with my mom.

•••

As I get older I have come to see many sub-species of stupid in the world and perhaps the dumbest I have yet to encounter is anyone in the know who decides to mess with my mom.

Now, understand, most people who interact with her see only a stooped-over diminutive grey-hair who has a wide smile and that little twinkle in her eye they mistake for girlish mischief. It is not.

It is a cold, calculating combat computer—what the Japanese call '*muga mushin*'—and while it might appear she is chuckling on some remembered innocent joke, she is probably thinking of a dozen ways to do you in.

Most of her interactions with the world are what would be considered normal and even pleasant. She has lots of friends in the neighborhood, is part of a little hen-pack of old ladies (who have no idea of her background as a government sanctioned mass murderer) and is highly thought of by the bag boys and check out folks at the local supermarket for her courtesy and tips.

However, when push comes to shove she shoves hardcore.

Such was the case the next morning when she took her little dog Banzai with her to a local bodega a couple of blocks from the house to get some scallions and doggie treats, and some chucklehead decided to make a grab for her purse.

If it had been just a snatch and grab artist I would not have given it much thought after the fact, and neither would she. He would have been acting because he believed the innocent act and she would have put him down without too much effort and minimal damage.

This guy should have known better as it was clear the second that Mom saw him he was yakuza, pure and simple. About five six, the guy was almost as wide as he was tall, all muscle and with a shaved head. The tattoo sleeves on his exposed arms were billboards of his criminal history.

He stepped out from behind a fruit display with a knife in his hand and grabbed the purse that she had slung across her shoulders. When he yanked on it the purse pulled her off balance and she actually dropped her cane as she reached out to steady herself against a shelf. She said later when we looked at the security tape from the bodega that her foot 'slipped' when she hit a wet spot but that was bunk—he caught her off guard, a fact I would not let her forget for a long time.

He then went straight for a throat slash with the heavy single-edged *tanto* he had. It would have been a fatal slash if it had struck home but Mom is a squirmy little bugger so as the blade came at her, instead of pulling away she dodged in toward the attacker.

He still had his left hand on the purse strap and she used that by winding the strap around his wrist and ducking so her head jammed with full force into his groin. She pulled down on the strap at the same time so he was thrown over her in a rough but effective *jiu jitsu* throw.

She squirmed out of the encumbering strap and grabbed a jar of pickles off the shelf behind her. When the thug started to climb to his feet she smacked him between the eyes with the heavy glass container and sent him falling backward with a cry of pain and a spray of blood.

While this was going on Banzai was losing his little dog mind, yapping and jumping all over the place. The bodega owner, who had been stacking shelves behind the counter, turned to see what the commotion was and his eyes went wide.

Mama-san bent, scooped up her dog, yelled *"Agarrar!"* in Spanish and tossed the confused pooch into the owner's hands.

The yakuza was on his feet again, blood pouring from his forehead over his right eye, partially blinding him so that he tried to wipe it away with his left hand while brandishing the *tanto* with his right. He started to move toward Mom while muttering a particularly foul Japanese curse.

Mom is old-fashioned in a lot of things and really doesn't like 'bad language.' Since she understood exactly what he was saying it only added fuel to the fire he had started. He really compounded his mistake in attacking her when he added, "Ghost Healer's Bitch" in Japanese, using the transliteration of my father's name.

Even when I watched the video of the fight afterward I could see my mother stiffen then giggle after he spoke.

That was a very bad sign: when Mom laughed like that she was full on *kunioshi*.

He lunged at her with the tanto, a bit clumsily because he was still trying to wipe blood from his eye. It didn't really matter though, because he could have glided in like Nureyev and she still would have done him darkly.

She sidestepped, grabbed his knife wrist in her tiny hands and executed the roughest, meanest wrist-twisting *kote-gaeshi* throw I have ever seen. Her whole body went into the torque that twisted his wrist, using his own momentum against him to send him flipping head over heels to slam into the floor.

She didn't stop there, however. During the throw she gave it some 'juice' and I imagine the sound of his wrist snapping was pretty loud. And when he hit the floor she jumped back while still holding the wrist that was enough strain to dislocate his shoulder.

He yelled like the damned which started Banzai barking again.

I will give it to the thug, he was as tough as he looked and twice as dumb because he grabbed the knife off the floor with his left hand and struggled to his knees to slash at her again.

This time she didn't mess around since it was clear he was dumber than a bucket of hammers. She spun around, slapped his hand inward toward him with her left, grabbed him at the elbow with the right and pulled.

He fell forward onto his knife, straight through his chest and didn't move again. He was done.

Mama-san didn't waste any time then, she went over and retrieved Banzai from the bodega owner, went behind the counter, removed the videotape from the machine and gave instructions to the owner what to tell the police when they showed up.

The owner stared at her but just nodded and obeyed, even breaking the videotape machine so he could say it had not been working. She bought him a new one the next day. Then she picked up her doggie treats, some scallions and went home.

Chapter Seven
NIP AND DUCK

"**D**id you really have to kill him?" I said to Mom when I looked at the videotape for the second time. She gave me the 'freeze hydrogen' stare that she does and when that didn't work, made a face.

"He used bad language," she said as explanation for signing him off.

"You were just pissed that you slipped."

"There was a wet spot," she said quickly then turned back to the sweater she was knitting for one of our relatives in Okinawa. Mom kept tabs on a vast network of family relations from both sides of the family through both open and encrypted channels, as half the family seemed to be in 'the game' either for governments or privately.

"Any blowback from this little jaunt?"

She didn't bother to look up. "I called that nice lady from Langley, Joyce, and told her there would be some mess to deal with and that it was connected to your work with them."

"So you lied."

"I stretched the truth," she was still intent on her knitting. "And who knows, it might be."

The local cops knew Mom but she liked to keep a low profile, so the bodega owner told them it was a crazy man that came in and threw himself around and then fell on his knife. They didn't believe a word of it, so they knew it was Mom, but there are advantages to having lots of CIA contacts. They can make anything go away with endowments to city governments.

"It could be an old enemy of yours or dad's too," I suggested. "You both crossed the Yamaguchi-gumi or any number of yakuza groups over the years."

Now she glanced up at me with her '*are-you-really-from-my-loins-you-complete-moron*,' look. "That was a clumsy attempt to kill me as a warning to you," she said. "Obviously. If it was revenge against me they would have killed you first."

I said her mind was a combat computer, but it was also as strategic as a master chess player. And often in things like murder she was right.

"So, it is an active case," I said. "Or recent."

"The girl." She said definitively and with disgust in her voice, "This is connected to her."

"You don't know that," I said but with the sinking feeling she was right. She gave me 'the look' again and went back to knitting.

My audience was over, so I gave Banzai a pat and went to the door but turned back before I left.

"Will you at least put the security system on?" I had installed a new system before I went over to Dubai and she had complained it was more complicated than the one I had installed before it. It wasn't, she just hated the idea that she might come to rely on the electronics to replace her own instincts.

"Yes, I will," she said, then added seriously, "I think this crazy girlfriend of yours is not good for you, Jonathan; but you are a man. You are your father's son. Anton had too big a heart as well and was as stubborn as you are. You will do what you do, but I say to be careful."

I was stunned by her statement and for a moment had no idea what to do or say. Then I bowed and said, "*Arigato gozaimashita, Okasama.*"

I was still feeling like I was in a dream when I left the house and headed to my car, parked down the block. Once I checked it for bombs (standard operating procedure all my life) I sat in it for a few minutes trying to take in what Mom had just said.

All my life I had lived in the shadow of my father who died when I was barely into my teens. He was a legendary do-gooder even before he was in the OSS when it started, then worked freelance for the CIA. All I ever heard was "Your father was—" from everyone.

It drove me away from his legacy and, I suppose Maria was something of an excuse for that. After the Corps I came to understand him more and came to realize I was my own man, but I never really felt that around Mom, who worshipped him. But, wow, what she said to me knocked me for a loop.

After a dozen deep breaths I pulled myself together and drove into the city to my place where I found a special delivery package from Joyce at Langley. It was an encrypted memory stick with the information I'd asked for. She had given me the encryption code for this specific drive so I would have access.

I pulled out an old laptop that was not wifi enabled and so was isolated and plugged the stick into it.

The information was much of what I had read in Myke's notes, in that Carter had vast world interests but with more concrete details about the rumored dealings with the yakuza. It said he had directly dealt with the Kobe Yamaguchi-gumi.

The Yamaguchi-gumi had been founded as a benevolent union or guild for Kobe dockworkers by Harukichi Yamaguchi around 1915.

Since then it had become one of the largest criminal organizations in the world with official members that numbered well over 55,000 and a reach beyond that of thousands more who were allied in some way. Just short of half of the 86,300 yakuza in the Japanese underworld owed them some form of allegiance.

They were among the world's wealthiest gangsters, bringing in billions of dollars a year from extortion, gambling, the sex industry, guns, drugs, and real estate and construction kickback schemes. They had also made a point of going 'upscale' by becoming involved in stock market manipulation and internet pornography.

When one of their members assassinated the mayor of Nagasaki in 2015 it led to a split and a schism in the group with the formation of the Kobe Yamaguchi-gumi.

According to the information from Joyce, that was when Carter began to pal around with the splinter group. The Kobe Yamaguchi-gumi operated all across Japan and had overseas operations in Asia and the United States.

"Dirty money always needs to get cleaned up somehow," I said as I flipped through the pages but the thing that really caught me was the newer pages. Two companies had just been placed on the UK sanctions list, one of which owned the land under the Yamaguchi-gumi headquarters in Kobe. In 2012 the Treasury Department of the United States announced sanctions and froze assets of the group; this year the government had upped the ante and added to the sanctions.

The sanctions froze any assets of those named that are under US jurisdiction and prohibited US individuals and companies from dealing with them. One of those companies was Carter's.

The last bit of interesting gristle to chew on was the fact that inside sources said that Carter and his companies and their connection with the Kobe Yamaguchi-gumi were on the verge of being investigated by the Securities and Exchange Commission. That level of scrutiny could cause all his assets to be frozen as well, making him a billionaire with no ready cash at all. And when the SEC gets on your tail jail time often follows the charges.

So Maria's getting out of the marriage may just be in time to avoid going to the pokie with hubby, I thought. *I need to know more about him and this car accident and where that money came from. I don't think there is any doubt the yakuza are in bed with him; the question is how far and exactly which faction.*

The illusion that the Japanese gangs were more civilized in dealings with partners than, say the Mafia or the Russian or Jamaican mobs was just that. It's true that each group of lowlife crooks had their own code of conduct, and the Japanese were nice and formal and all, but when push came to shove they would shiv you without blinking an eye. They were bad people to be in bed with.

I took the thumb drive and wiped it, cleaned the laptop and got myself an ice pop while I stared out the window and watched someone walking their dog in the park.

I tried not to think about Mom and Banzai but watching the miniature city dog tugging on the leash of the little old lady in the park made that not possible. Mama-san was right, again; getting involved with Maria and her husband had to have brought the yakuza thug down on her.

But how had they known? Was Maria being followed and they saw me save her? Had someone I asked questions of spread the word, or worse been bugged?

Not Myke. Not Joyce.

So she was followed.

So it was deliberate hit on her.

That changed things a bit; quite a bit.

Chapter Eight
HEARTH AND HOMICIDE

I was busy digesting the information I'd gotten about Carter's ties to the Japanese underworld and the coming possible investigation and wanted to ask Maria questions about it so I got into my car and headed upstate. It didn't hurt that I knew I'd arrive in time for Sammo to make one of his awesome lunches for me to eat.

I was only about ten minutes outside of Walden when I got a red alert text from Sammo. It was a family code that meant things were critical. A simple symbol that meant many things, including don't call—just come ready to fight!

"Crap!" I hit the gas hard and pushed my car through traffic up the turnpike with a sick feeling in the pit of my stomach. Sammo was not the panic button type; a red alert from him was a DEFCON 4 situation. I pulled my Glock semi-automatic from the glove compartment and a spare clip and put both in my jacket pocket as I drove.

I also sent a text to Mom to tell her I was going in hot and would get back to her. She would be ready to alert some of her old contacts if Sammo and I needed help. I might not have gone that far with anyone else, but Sammo was not an alarmist and he had his house rigged like a fort so I had to expect a mess.

With what I had learned about the yakuza connection and with my suspicions that Maria had been followed to me it was possible they had somehow been able to tail me up to his place; I cursed myself to have been distracted enough to maybe have made that possible.

I had to slow down when I got into town, parked two blocks away from Sammo's and headed through the backyard of his neighbor's to come at the house from behind the dojo building.

At his property line I stopped and took stock.

The house was on a slight rise almost in the center of the land but with the greenery cleared into a wide lawn to give Sammo a clear field of fire from the house. So even if none of the electronic systems were working, crossing the open space in broad daylight was going to be a chore if anyone was looking.

I knew an electronic-free corridor that led me to the back of the dojo—a sort of 'back door' that Sammo built in when he designed the system. Like I said, layers of onions in onions. One always has to plan for a way to overcome your own system in the event the bad guys get control. Ninjas are devious folk and we really try to figure all the angles.

The 'back door' was a convoluted crawling path that zig-zagged through the brush to take me right up to the dojo. When I moved to the hidden switch to turn off the alarm to the outbuilding I was concerned to see that it was already deactivated, so I slipped inside and locked the door behind me.

Once in the room (I did not take off my shoes even though a lifetime of training in martial arts schools made me think about it for a second) I made my way to the small window that let me take a clear look at the house.

I could see no activity. No movement at all at any of the windows, but then I could only see the kitchen and dining room on the first floor, and some of the guest bedrooms on the second and third floors.

"Okay, Sammo," I whispered. "What is it all about?" While I kept my eyes glued to the house I reached into one of my cousin's weapon racks and got an antique WWII era Ka-Bar knife in a scabbard. I slipped the scabbard on my belt and made the decision that I would have to chance a run across the open space to the house. I was about to open the door just as there was a development.

The kitchen door opened and two guys looked very professional in black

...and put both in my pocket...

battle dress uniforms. They had silenced Heckler and Koch MP 5 sub-machine guns on combat slings. They came down the stairs, obviously heading for the dojo building with a relaxed, but alert attitude.

My mind was racing and I had a cold feeling in the pit of my stomach worrying about Maria being in that house, but I pushed that thought down, locking it away in the place where emotions had to be put when I was 'working.' *"Be professional, "Mama-san always said. Professionals have no feelings."*

I went to the weapons rack and grabbed Sammo's short recurve bow and a handful of arrows then moved swiftly to the door to listen.

Outside the two men stopped.

"I thought all the alarms are off," one of the men said to the other in Japanese as they donned gasmasks.

"Yeah, I know," the second man replied in Japanese in what I thought sounded like a Kobe accent, as if I needed more clues to who they were, "but that dog-eater is sneaky. Boss said to not take chances there aren't also mechanical booby traps; we have to make the search thorough." He slipped on his mask and as I watched reached for the doorknob into the dojo.

I raced back across the room and ducked down behind the archery butt target. One of the skills I studied was speed shooting, so I took four arrows and held them between the fingers of my left hand and nocked one of the shafts.

The two jiggled the doorknob a couple of times and then they kicked the door in, coming in low and with the guns ready for trouble. They were very professional, spreading to either side of the door to sweep the room.

I waited until they were looking at opposite sides of the room then popped up and sent two shafts through the left eyepiece of one of the men. Before the second guy could react I sent two more into him, one at the throat and one struck a glancing blow off the eyepiece but did not penetrate the glass lens.

The arrows didn't drop him and he moved to swing the gun at me, getting off two shots before I put one last arrow into the eyepiece, this time doing the job, the mass of the shaft pushing it through the lens and into his brain. He dropped like a broken puppet.

I was across the room almost before he hit the ground and cleared the weapons from the two of them and checked; they were both very dead.

I took the HP5 from one of them and then jumped to the door to watch outside.

There was no more action at the house.

I did a quick search of the bodies but there were no wallets or identifying documents. I rolled one over and used the Ka-Bar to cut open the shirt, ripping it wide enough to see the tattoos on his back to be certain.

"Yakuza!" It was no wonder they were so professional; I knew the gangs maintained strike teams to do hits and raids—they had grown very professional when it came to killing enemies.

Now I was really worried about Sammo.

I took a couple of spare magazines from the dead men and, ducking low, ran for the house.

I made it to the back stoop without getting fired on and hugged the cool stone of the foundation. I listened hard. Not a sound.

Damn, Sammo, I thought. I ran around the building, keeping low below the window line and hopped up onto the front veranda. Out front on the circular driveway I could see two dark SUVs besides Sammo's, parked to block his car, so potentially there could be as many as eight or ten men inside. *A regular assault force!*

The windows from the veranda were big on the front of the house so I could peer in to get a view of the living room, dining room, the staircase to the second floor and a little piece of the library. The window was cracked open a bit (there was a failsafe that let Sammo open it for air about two inches) but there was no sound from inside; it was eerily quiet.

The place looked like a tornado had gone through it with overturned furniture, drawers pulled out and holes in the walls in several places.

They were looking for something, I thought, *or someone.*

I had a chill again thinking about Maria, but I knew Sammo would have gotten her into one of the panic rooms at the first sign of any trouble.

Keep your mind on the job; stay professional.

I was just about to move to the front door when I saw movement on the slice of the stairs I could see. There were two more black-clad intruders, coming down the steps, their attitude casual.

They also spoke in Japanese. "Yukio and Hanzo had better get a move on so the four of us can get out of here," the taller man said. "I know we have a half hour at least, but I don't like to push it. Shadowsama is no one to tangle with if you can help it."

"Scared of a half-breed?" the second man asked.

"This one, yes, Kenzo," the tall one said. "He's his mother's son."

While I was flattered to be feared the takeaway was that there were four intruders, two now dead and no doubt that the attack was targeted.

I watched the two men move out of sight heading toward the back of the house and decided I had to act. I levered up the window and dropped into the living room and moved quickly toward the stairs.

Which hidey-hole are you in, Sammo? I thought. *And where did you stash Maria?*

I hugged the hallway wall, aware of the two intruders who could return from the back of the house at any time. I knew there was a small panic room hidden behind a shelf in the pantry off the kitchen, and one upstairs off Sammo's office, disguised as a shallow closet. It was clear they had been punching holes searching for something, and I had to assume it was for my cousin and Maria.

I had no idea how they breached Sammo's security, but the fact that there were no dead intruders scattered around made me assume that my cousin chose to hide with Maria rather than fight.

So I hoped he was upstairs.

I started up the steps stealthily, my attention still on the kitchen where I could hear the two yakuza sounding out the walls. That was why I missed the guy coming down the stairs!

Chapter Nine
THE HIDDEN AND THE HORROR

The guy at the top of the stairs was looking behind him saying "I'll tell the others that—" then he screamed "Shadowsama!" when he stepped onto the top step and saw me.

I had no choice but to fire from the hip with the silenced HP5, giving a three-bullet burst right through the guy's center of mass.

He came tumbling down toward me and I raced up as fast as I could, knowing my gunshots had been heard in the kitchen and the other two would come running.

The dead guy slammed into me and almost unbalanced me so that I stumbled and had to grab the handrail to keep from falling. In doing so I had to drop the HP5.

I shrugged off the falling thug and sprinted up the steps just as the two from the kitchen got to the bottom of the staircase and let loose with a fusillade of bullets. I was close enough to the top to dive to the landing, rolling and pulling my Glock.

I spun to fire down at the two but at the same time perceived movement over my left shoulder.

I had really screwed up.

I rolled over to see a shocked yakuza trying to get his own gun off a back strap to shoot at me. I stopped that with a double tap to his head.

I heard a crackle of a radio below without being able to make out the words and the guys at the bottom of the stairs had backed off their fire. When I turned back to them the gunfire stopped all together.

I hugged the wall near the stairs with my head on a swivel while I listened hard to anyone else upstairs or any sign of any of activity downstairs.

I knew there was a set of servant stairs near the kitchen so I had to worry they were trying to flank me. I held my breath and waited. And waited.

In only a few minutes I heard a car start up and drive off outside.

What the hell? They had my ass if they'd split up on me.

I waited for a few minutes more but there was no more activity or sound, so I grabbed the fallen guy's MP5 and went down again to check out the front. One of the SUVs was gone.

They pulled out! I was stunned. I did a sweep of the first floor, checking the hideaway in the kitchen, which was empty. That meant that if Sammo and Maria didn't run they would be upstairs.

I went up the servant stairs still cautious in case I had grossly screwed up twice and there was a trap. There wasn't any.

I came out of the back hallway into the one where the closet hid the safe room and stopped short. There was a body laying on the floor just in front of the closet.

It was a stocky figure with dark hair dressed in a silk happy coat over sweatpants. There was a splotch of dried blood on the back of the head and a pool of blood spreading and drying from under the head.

I knew.

I knew without turning the body over that it was Dae Hoon.

Dead.

My cousin, my friend, my companion in so many adventures silly and serious, was dead.

Really dead with a bullet hole in the back of his head.

Of course they got him from behind, I thought. *Nobody could take Sammo face to face.*

I swallowed hard and had to will myself to move past him. I could not make myself look down at the body; flashbacks of his smiling, full-of-life face came unbidden and I had to force them away. It was clear he was dead, no reason to check further and look into his dead face. *Stay professional. Stay professional!*

The way he was stretched out it was as if he had been heading toward the closet where the safe room was hidden.

Maria!

I opened the closet that looked just like that, a shallow space with a few coats, a golf bag and a couple of cardboard boxes. Pointless things, purposely chosen to be ordinary.

I stepped in and pressed on a hidden switch in the back. There was an almost soundless hiss and the back of the closet slid aside to reveal a safe door.

I punched in the code and the safe door swung aside. Beyond was a six-by-six-foot room that had been built into a space between two other rooms but invisible from either of them.

The door opened and there was Maria. She cowered against the far wall, holding a bottle of soda like a club and with an expression of fear on her face such as I had never seen on anyone, certainly not on her.

"Jon!" she yelled and all but collapsed into my arms. "I was terrified when Dae Hoon locked me in. He said he'd be right back but it's been so long and the close circuit TVs don't work so I had no idea what was going on. Where is he?" The words exploded out of her in one long burst and then she started to sob on my shoulder.

"Easy, Maria," I said, doing my best to stay professional. "We have to grab your stuff and get out of here, fast."

"Get out?" She said, "Where is Dae Hoon?"

"They got him when he was on the way back into the safe room."

"No!" She sobbed and I had to grip her by the shoulders. "No."

"You have to get your stuff now," I said in my command voice. She did her best to pull herself together at the order.

"We have to leave right away." I took her by the hand and led her past my cousin's body to the staircase. I stopped to take some extra clips for the MP5 from one of the bodies at the bottom. I ran around and closed all the windows and pulled the shades down, locked the front door then headed for the back.

"Wait, one minute," I said to Maria at the back door. "I'll be right back—"

"No, don't leave me," she said.

"Stay!" I said forcefully. "I'll only be a moment." She looked hurt but listened and did not move.

Stay professional, I chided myself, fighting the desire to sweep her up into my arms and comfort her. *This has to be done.*

I ran to Sammo's office, going directly to the antique desk he used. I reached under it to the hidden switch that sprung a shallow secret drawer. In it were two thumb drives, some papers, two glass vials, several of his 'alternate' passports and about ten thousand dollars in cash. I took the cash and the thumb drives then broke the glass vials and slammed the drawer closed. The released acid would destroy all the documents and passports. Hopefully he didn't have another cache in the house I didn't know of, but both of us were well trained to destroy family records and secret information and to keep each other informed. We were Frick and Frack, despite our ages, as close as brothers, and as selfish as it was I could not imagine life without him. *What the hell am I gonna do for back up now, Cuz?*

Stay professional!

I ran back to Maria, fighting the urge to look back up toward the stairs, picturing Sammo's body in my mind.

I made it back to Maria.

"Let's go!" I said and grabbed her hand.

We exited out the back door, raced through the woods and back to my vehicle. Once we were in the car I didn't let myself rest, but started it up and drove off and headed for the highway.

Only after we were moving did either of us speak.

"What happened back there?" I asked. I tried not to make it sound accusing, but I am sure my anxiety made the question sound harsh.

"What do you mean?"

"I mean, tell me what happened, exactly."

She took a deep breath and said, "I was in my room reading and your cousin came racing in. He told me to come and then pulled me along the hallway and put me in that safe room. 'Stay here till Jon or I come to get you.' Then he closed the door. I tried to get the monitors to work but they wouldn't. I was going crazy waiting but I knew better than to come out till he told me to." She started to break down, crying. "All those dead men..."

"Take it easy," I said. "We'll sort this all out."

"What are we going to do, where are we going?"

"We're going to go 'ghost,'" I said. "To hide until we have to be at the annual meeting."

"But Dae Hoon..." she managed between sobs, "He—"

"First, I have to get to a land line for me to call my mother." It was a call I didn't relish making. "Then we have to find a way to get different wheels and disappear."

I looked into the rearview mirror and imagined Sammo's face looking back at me. *See you on the other side!* I thought. *Maybe sooner than later, Cuz.*

Chapter Ten
GHOST INTERLUDE

We stopped at a diner on Route 17 and I put a call in to Mama-san from a payphone booth outside. I spoke in the mountain Korean dialect that my dad had always used with his core group of helpers; I'd learned it as a kid and had to be careful not to use it when I spoke to Korean relatives because it was considered 'yokel talk.' It was so thick that even many Koreans could not understand it; hence it worked as a sort of secret code. I had inherited my father's ability with language and it had come in handy many times.

The call to Mom was the hardest thing I ever had to do, the words I had to say to tell her about Dae Hoon the hardest I have ever had to say.

She greeted those words with stony silence. After I said he was dead I described everything that happened from what Maria told me to all I had done. She remained silent the entire time, letting me finish the story before she spoke up.

"That woman is a curse," she said in a harsh whisper, but then she went back to all business. "You did right to destroy what you did and seal the house. I will call Dave Burton in the NSA to send a cleaning crew to the house; they will remove all evidence. I am sure they can have a team there within a few hours." She was silent for a long moment then added, "I assume they will make Dae Hoon's death seem a death by an electrical fire and smoke inhalation and provide the legal papers to prove it."

"I am worried about his boyfriend Robert returning unexpectedly; he will have to be found and diverted." I told her where he was and started to tell her where his address could be found in an old-fashioned Rolodex on the desk at her place.

"I will see to it," Mama-san said. "Your cousin left his friend's information with me as well." She cleared her throat and it was the first indication that she had been crying—something my mother seldom did. It choked me up to think of it. "I will call Suki and also Dae Hoon's father and tell them."

"*Haha*," I said, using the most formal Japanese for mother. "I had no way of knowing that—"

"Do not make excuses," she cut me off, "What is done is done. You must stay professional. You must find out how these tattooed men found the house. And you must stay vigilant so you may stay alive."

"Yes," I said, "I had thought of that. I will take the usual steps." I heard her grunt in an affirmative. As much as we fought, I knew she was aware of my ability in the game and did not discount it.

"There is much to be done," she said with finality. "I will begin; be professional and come home to me."

"I will, *Haha*," I said. "And I will find out why Dae Hoon died and punish those responsible."

"*Honto*," she said and hung up.

She had to put a dig in. *Honto* means essentially, 'Oh Really' but then I deserved it—I got Sammo into the mess. Maria was sitting in the car outside the phone booth watching me on the phone and I could see concern written on her face.

I certainly understood her concern. We were in the wind now; somehow the assassins had found her and until we figured out how, we were vulnerable to another attack. I still had no proof that the attack on Sammo was all about Maria. It could have been an old grudge against Dae Hoon or any member of my family, but the coincidence of it was a pretty strong case for it being connected to her husband, especially since the killers where yakuza. And I learned a long time ago that there were really no coincidences in the game when death was involved.

The killers knew me and my family, had taken Dae Hoon's life and tried to kill my mother so it *was* personal now whether or not it had started with Maria's husband. There would be no end to it till I found out who commanded the drones to attack us and I killed them. I had no illusions. It would not go away. There would be no negotiation. From this point on there was going to be a lot of spilled blood and my heart was hardened to that fact.

This is going to be a hell of a fight, Cuz, I thought to Dae Hoon. *I would have no doubts about it with you to back me, Sammo, but now? Now I will do what I have to, but it is no sure thing without you. Damn, how the hell did anyone out sneak you, Cuz?*

That was the thing that still stuck in my craw; how could they get past Sammo's security system? He was not careless; if anything, he was more careful than I was. How could he be surprised?

They had known there were panic rooms, they had to. The thing that tipped it for me was the fact that the two I killed in the dojo seemed like they were searching for something or someone specific. And once again that seemed to place it at Maria's feet.

"Maybe she *is* cursed," I whispered to myself, "or maybe *we* are."

"What?" Maria said as I slipped into the car after the phone call.

"Nothing," I said, "Just thinking out loud."

"What did your mother say?"

"Nothing good," I said. "But it got me thinking. If those guys came after you they had to know you were there. Their information was just too specific. The question is, how?"

"But I didn't know where I was going when you brought me up," Maria said.

"You made no phone calls? Contacted no one on line?"

"No, I thought it better to stay offline," she said. "Remember I know what kind of data mining can be done. And no phone calls." She gave a mirthless laugh. "It was good to unplug and just read and listen to music."

I sat for a long moment and thought. We needed a real plan or we'd blunder into trouble again. Maria was good about not interrupting me or asking questions. She just reached over and rested a hand on my arm in a reassuring gesture. I have to admit it felt good, better than it had a right to considering the horror we had just left behind us.

"Okay," I finally said after about ten minutes of staring out the window. "Here is what we are going to do. We're going to go into the thrift store in town and buy some clothes, then ditch everything you're wearing, including underwear."

"What? Why?"

"We have to assume there is a possibility that you had some sort of tracker on you; you know how small they can be. I don't have equipment with me to scan for it so we eliminate the possibility. And a wig. That thrift store doesn't have a camera, but other places will have later. So hats and wigs are a thing now."

"You're serious."

"Dead." I said. "We have to fall off the map. Cash only for things, avoiding cameras when we can. Gotta ditch this car as soon as we can get to a used car lot and get a junker to move around in."

I was lucky I had a cover I.D. with me in a sealed packet hidden in the upholstery of the car; like I said, ninjas always have layers within layers. I had a cutoff credit card in that identity and a burner phone if I needed it as well. "And we stay in the wind until we have to go to that meeting; ghosting in order not to end up being turned into real ghosts."

"Whatever you say," Maria said. "You know this world, I don't."

"Unfortunately, I do," I said.

We didn't say anything more as I drove into Newburgh, a town along the Hudson that used to be an escape for the rich with mansions on the river front and workers' houses moving inland. Now it was gentrified near the river but an economically depressed town with lots of secondhand and thrift stores. I stayed with the car while Maria, wearing a hoodie I had in the car, went in and bought new clothes for herself, some clothes for me and two suitcases for when we chose to check into a motel at some point.

"You changed everything, even the underwear?" I asked. "And left them behind?"

"I couldn't bear to buy underwear in a secondhand place," she said. "So I'm going without until I can buy new at another store; or is that TMI?"

"Fair enough," I said with a laugh. "Once we change cars then we can breathe a bit easier."

On the way out of town I found a small car dealership and was able to buy a 'second car for my younger sister' for cash and I was able to get insurance online with the fake ID I had with me. The dealer plate let Maria drive it behind me and we moved on to the little town of Pine Bush, about fifteen minutes away from Newburgh.

Pine Bush was another 'Americana' type town that had the distinction of having been the home of the Grand Dragon of the Klu Klux Klan in the northeast in the 90s and a hot spot of UFO activity since the 1970s. They even have a UFO festival every year to celebrate that fact.

We missed the festival, darn!

We found a small motel just outside town, parked the junker around the corner then checked into the motel using my real car's license. I also used my credit card to pay for a week in advance. That would establish me as at that motel if anyone was looking for me and I hoped it worked as a red herring. If we were lucky they would stake out the motel and waste their time waiting for us.

We parked my car at the rear of the motel and let ourselves be seen going in to our room with one of the empty suitcases. I stripped down and put on the thrift store clothes on the off chance I had been the one tagged and my visit two days ago had been the one who brought the assassins to Sammo's place. The only problem was the sneakers she got me were half a size too small, but I'd get better ones the next day.

After fifteen minutes we slipped out quietly, put the 'do not disturb' sign on the door and slunk away unseen to make our way to the junker.

We drove out of town in the junker and headed across the border into Jersey. The temporary dealer's plate would give us at least a week before I'd have to figure out what to do.

It was dark by the time we checked into a trucker's motel. We bought new clothes, country western chic, at the store attached to the motel and ate a simple but pretty good meal at the attached restaurant. All with cash.

All this time we had said very little with me running the events of the day over and over in my head and trying to lay out a plan for the next week. As for Maria, I imagine she was a little shocked by the rapidity of it all.

When dinner was done, however the fact that we had both been avoiding was painfully clear; we would be in the same motel room together for the first time in twenty-two years.

We walked slowly toward the second floor acutely aware that even after all that happened that day we were about to enter a room and confront feelings that should, by all rights, not be allowed to come alive again.

Stay professional and stay alive, stay professional!

Fat chance.

Chapter Eleven
INTERLUDE AND INTENSITY

When I slid the bolt on the inside of the hotel room I felt like I was nineteen years old again. I had butterflies in my stomach and I felt a little light-headed. While I should have been thinking about my dead cousin, the squad of killer Japanese gangsters trying to kill me and a mother who thought I was insane, I was thinking about the woman behind me and my pulse was racing.

Stay professional, I thought but then I turned around to see Maria putting her things in one of the dressers and my breath caught in my throat.

"I'll take this bed," she said as she sat on the one that was farthest from the door. "Its closer to the bathroom." She sat back, kicked off her new/used sneakers and sighed. "Not too bad for a fleabag motel; you weren't kidding about keeping a low profile. This is pretty low."

"Not the Ritz, for sure," I said sitting on my own bed and purposely looking away from her. "Truckers' places are always basic, but clean and neat. And we can get you better clothes tomorrow at the mall and we can eat well for the next few days. I think we had better not stay in one place more than two nights at a time though. At the end of the week we can drive directly up to your husband's place."

"I already think of him as my ex-husband," she said. There was an odd hitch in her voice as she added. "I think of myself as a free woman these days."

I pulled off the painful sneakers, massaging my pained toes and made a mental note for new shoes to be the first thing after breakfast. I did my best not to read anything into her statement.

"You will be when we serve those papers on William," I said. "Just hold onto that fact." I didn't say that I knew that wouldn't be the end of it; it would just be the beginning of it for me because I would not stop until I made sure every single son-of-a-bitch who had anything to do with Dae Hoon's death was rotting in hell.

I lay back on the bedspread with my head against the headboard and my eyes closed. I tried to get the image of Sammo's body out of my mind's eye. Aloud I said, "we should be pretty good as far as ghosting is concerned, but when we switch to the next motel we'll go a little more upstate, I think, that way we—"

There was a sudden weight on the bed and I jumped, my hand going for my Glock before my eyes snapped open to see Maria kneeling next to me, looking startled.

"I'm sorry," she said then burst into tears. "I didn't mean to...I just thought..." She jumped back off the bed and headed for the bathroom.

"Maria!" I called, "I'm sorry, its okay, you just startled me."

She stopped at the doorway and looked at me over her shoulder, her face a mask of conflicting emotions as she fought back tears. "I just...I was scared, Jon and thought..."

I walked over to her and pulled her into my arms. She melted into me, her head against my chest and the warmth of her made me feel like my skin was on fire.

"I need you, Jon," she whispered. "I don't mean to be weak but...but I need you."

I felt myself spiral inside. My defenses deflated like a punctured balloon and all my professional attitude went out the window. The memories of her turning me away after college, my pain at feeling the fool for loving her so much, the time in the bottle, even my failed marriage all disappeared in her touch, the scent of her perfume and the taste of her lips.

The next hour was a blur of animal passion.

I was nineteen again and she was the center of the world, my hope for the future and proof to me that I was man enough to take on the world on my own terms—something not easy to do with a legendary father and mother who could kick Muhammad Ali's ass.

My rational mind still protested, weakly, at first. *She's married; she's a client; because of her Sammo is dead; you have to stay alert for ambush,* but all of those objections were swept away in the flood of passion that over-whelmed the two of us.

Years of repressed and averted lust on my part, as well as all the dreams I'd had when she had first dumped me so hard that I fell into the bottle, foamed up to the surface in me and in her arms I found myself floating on a wave of retro feelings.

Maria answered my passion with her own, fueled, I was sure, by her insecurity and fear. I know mine was fired by so many conflicting emotions I was not quite sure where I was most of the time.

And, frankly at that moment I didn't care. I was holding Maria and she was holding me and that was all that mattered.

To hell with the rest of the world!

When our passion was finally spent we lay in our own sweat. The bed-clothes were a tangled mess all around us. We clung to each other as if afraid to let go, as if it were all some sort of dream that we would wake from.

"Jon," she whispered after a while.

"Shh," I said. "We don't need words."

"No, I have to say it," she insisted. "I...I feel a fool for all those years ago, but I honestly—"

"That was then. This is now. Maybe only now, but nonetheless it is *now*. We were different people then. Who we are now is what matters."

"I just want you to know," fear in her voice, "I am still unsure about who I will be when I am free of William. I...I have lived in fear for so long; he was so angry for so long...even before the accident. Then...then after the scar-ring from the crash he got violent. I may need time alone or...I don't know..."

"It is okay. I am not asking for tomorrow. Right now is good enough. It means we begin everything new going forward. A fresh start. We didn't even have that before. So if I have to wait a bit to see what kind of butterfly you become, I will."

She made a face. "You calling me a worm, fella?"

"That's a caterpillar. I thought you computer heads were supposed to be smart."

"I'm at idiot-savant, okay," she gave me a relieved smile. "Right now though, I am interested in your worm."

•••

I called Mama-san from a phone booth when we had moved on the second day to a second little motel about fifty miles north of Newburgh again. It is amazing how many little mom and pop motels are up in that area so we had no problem disappearing again.

"Dave Burton's people took care of the mess," Mom said in a neutral tone. "The yakuza will be made to disappear—they proved to be very low-level soldiers of the Kobe Yamaguchi-gumi faction and were in the U.S. illegally. Your cousin's death was recorded as a kitchen fire and smoke inhalation, but it was done with minimal damage to the house and all signs of the bullet damage were made to disappear as well so the house can be given to Dae Hoon's partner, Robert; it was in your cousin's will."

"That is good," I said. "Robert made him happy and from the times I met him he seemed a good man. Knowing he is taken care of would make Dae Hoon happy."

"You finding out who ordered this will make him happy," my mother said sharply. "Now what is being done with that girl?"

There it was. I took a deep breath knowing my mother was sure to read micro-tones in my voice to tell exactly what *had* been happening with Maria.

"We are going to her husband's place in three days to serve the papers. It seems to be what this is all about and the only way I see to move forward is to play it out and I will see in what direction this goes."

"Have you let that girl distract you?" My mother was always very direct. And I knew she already knew what had happened.

"No!" I answered too quickly. She snorted.

"I am staying professional," I added.

"How will you get where you are going?"

"We originally had a flight from upstate New York out of Stewart Airport. Before the attack at Sammo's we would have flown separately into Buffalo Airport and then rented a car, but airports are under too much scrutiny for people trying to ghost."

"So you will drive?"

"Yes. Doing it in stages, staying at small motels off the beaten path." There was a moment of silence and I knew what she was thinking so I added as an olive branch, "Just like you taught me."

"Stay professional," my mother insisted once more but her order seemed softened. "Do not let her distract you, Jonathan."

"I won't, *Haha,* I promise." I hung up.

I stood there breathing hard for a minute staring at the phone. She was right, of course, she always was—I could not afford to let my feelings for Maria distract me, and I would not. I had to let what had happened be the last time until—until it was all over. I had to be hyper vigilant from this

...we lay in our own sweat.

point out. If the Kobe Yamaguchi-gumi or her husband were looking for us they knew we were going to head to his place, The Lair, and had only two ways to get there; fly or drive.

It would not take too many men to cover the airports, but if I kept to the back roads and took the long way around we might just evade any ad hoc dragnet.

As it was, it was all I could do to keep Maria safe. And I *would* keep her safe.

I could not—I couldn't lose Maria this time. We had a real chance and so the stakes were higher than they ever had been.

And I still had to find out who put the thugs on Sammo and make them pay in full!

Chapter Twelve
WENT TO A GARDEN PARTY

"If you don't keep your eyes on the road, Maria, you'll kill both of us before your husband has a chance to," I warned as Maria swerved the car for the third time in ten minutes because she had gestured too violently while talking.

"I'm Italian," she apologized. "I can't help it." There was not a doubt of Italian descent by the fact that she kept taking her hands off the wheel to make strangling motions whenever she talked about her soon to be ex-husband William Carter. In the last two days, even though we had not repeated our lustful catharsis she nonetheless was more relaxed and even understanding of my reluctance to reengage.

And I felt more relaxed as well; not that it made sense, but I felt that there was hope now that we really might have a chance together in the future. The distant future. In the meantime, my head was clear and I felt focused. We would serve her husband and then I would follow the threads to the people that had taken Sammo down. Then; then I'd look at time with Maria again. Until then we lived in a bubble of promise and that was better than the fear from before. We had even slept in separate beds so I'd be more alert but it had been surprisingly not awkward; and that made me hopeful. Maria was stronger than her old self, and so was I.

"Well, then let me drive," I offered again. For the third time. She had taken over for me at the last rest stop to let me 'relax,' she said.

We drove a couple of hours north, then east, and had rented another car under my cover identity for the last leg of the drive up to her husband's pseudo-baronial estate called 'The Lair' on the US/Canadian border. I'd driven most of the way but after a time she wanted to drive saying she got carsick as a passenger for long drives.

"You were fine yesterday," I reminded her.

"It wasn't that long a drive," she insisted, "besides, we are close enough now and I know the way, on these back roads…all the short cuts." When I looked at her she shrugged. "I'm getting antsy doing nothing; this will occupy my mind."

"That mind of yours is never idle, Maria, I'll let you get away with it this time; but I warn you I might begin to sing with no wheel in my hands to keep me busy." I wasn't really all that impatient, but it didn't hurt to distract her; Maria had always been high-strung at college. Even though we had been comfortable the last couple of days, I had noticed in the last few hours she seemed to have a growing anxiety as we approached her husband's place. With everything and the horror of Sammo's death it was understandable.

The upstate New York countryside was lovely, wooded and with hilly vistas coming up surprisingly around turns. We were not on the new highways now, but rather back roads. It was an all-together peaceful trip; but I should have realized it was too peaceful.

When we were only minutes out from her husband's estate and I was dozing a bit, Maria braked hard as she was coming around a turn and fishtailed to a stop on the macadam road.

"What the f—" I began but shut up when I saw why she had almost sent me through the windshield—there was a huge branch from a tree that had fallen across the road. If I'd been driving with my usual lead foot we might have hit it hard. It was practically a small tree on it own and it completely blocked the passage.

"Sorry, Jon."

"Nothing to be sorry about. There was a storm up here a couple of days ago." I got out of the car and took a quick survey of the tree and realized I'd have to wrestle it out of the way if we didn't want to chance the bushes on the shoulder of the road. It was good sized and there would be some effort involved.

I shed my shoulder holster, tossing it into the car and rolled up my sleeves. "Just give me a minute to do my Hercules act," I quipped as I pushed my way through the bushy branches of the fallen limb to get a grip on the trunk. Just as I bent over to grip the tree the thugs attacked.

There were three of them. They were ski-masked and were dressed head to foot in camouflaged BDUs.

All three were wielding graphite billy clubs and they came in at me swinging hard.

Three things saved me from a split skull. One; I never completely let my guard down, even with physical memory of the post-coitus cloud of endorphins swirling around me—it was something Mama-san drilled into me early on in life.

Secondly, the tree branch they had felled made any direct attack impossible because of the mad foliage and thickness of the limb and lastly, it is one of the immutable truths of the universe that multiple attackers always get in each other's way.

The first attacker swung a haymaker that would have decapitated me if I hadn't ducked. I let his momentum from the swing expose his right side to me than I drove a knife-hand blow to his floating rib. He doubled over and cursed in Japanese.

Attacker two was a little less enthusiastic but still swung a club at my head. I let him swing, leaned back to avoid the billy and front kicked him in his future generations. His curses were epic.

Attacker three, on the other side of the tree from me said, 'Baka Yamero yo! (Stop being idiots!) Ima watashitachiha On'nanoko o eru koto ga deki-nai!" (Now we can't get the girl!). He reached into his shirt and pulled a semi-automatic pistol and aimed it at me. "Neji no juchou!" (Screw orders!)

I barely had time to reflect on my misspent life (or how three Japanese thugs had found me to attack me in the woods of New York) before there was the cough of a gun behind me and number three fell over backwards with a bullet between his eyes.

I spun around to see Maria holding my Glock in a perfect Weaver stance.

I ran back to her shouting, "Get into the passenger seat!" as I jumped behind the wheel, reached over to bodily pulled her into the car, took the gun away from her and floored it.

I sure as hell blew the security deposit on the rental car when I raced up onto the shoulder and scraped my way around the tree, kicking up dirt as I did.

"What the hell was that?" Maria asked in a strained voice. Her eyes were wild and she was hyperventilating.

"Not a plain old robbery," I answered. We were back on the road but I didn't slow down. "They were waiting for us; you can bet they felled that branch knowing we were going to be coming up this road."

"It had to be William. He would guess I would take this way to his place," she said with venom. "Now you see why I want you along. I'll bet he planned for me to crash and…and those men would have…" Her dark eyes began to tear up and she started to sob, her shoulders jumping with the effort.

"Easy, Maria. This only proves that the attack at Dae Hoon's was part of a pattern: these guys were Japanese as well, a sure bet they were Kobe Yamaguchi-gumi variety yakuza."

My attention was split between the road ahead, the rearview mirror and glancing at her. Even sniffling she still looked good.

Despite my hard-nosed attitude I knew it is not an easy thing to take a human life, even a stranger whose face you could not see in the heat of battle. I had been trained my whole life, raised with the idea that you killed the enemy and I still remember the first life I was forced to take when a Hajji came at me in an alley in Fallujah. I still saw his face some nights just before I nodded off to sleep as clearly as the moment I watched the light of his life fade out of his eyes.

They say it gets easier to kill after the first one and in a sense it does; once you know your life does go on once you kill, and you know there is something after the bullets fly or the bloody knife is withdrawn. I still saw all the faces, fading in the shadows of my thoughts, not as clearly as that first one, but clear enough to see the humanity I had taken from them.

I have never taken a life if circumstances allowed for some other answer, but I also knew the decision had to be snap, had to be in the moment and had to assume the other guy was trying to take my life first. That is all that allowed me to sleep, knowing if I had hesitated any of those times I would not be around to help people like Maria. The ghosts still floated into my dreams—sometimes waking ones—but I was on speaking terms with them.

Not so with Maria. The reality of what she had done was beginning to set in on her and all the civilized world's training against taking life, against the violence she had just perpetrated was beginning to well up from within her.

"Where did you learn to shoot like that, Annie Oakley?" I tried to keep her talking to distract her.

Her sobs had stopped and she answered me almost calmly. "You can thank William's paranoia for my shooting. He insisted I learn how to shoot to defend myself and hired some ex-cop to teach the two of us. Before the accident, before he stopped caring—" She stopped abruptly and I thought she was going to start crying again. "That was before he decided he didn't care what happened to me at all."

"I don't think that's the case anymore. Judging from the reception committee I'd say he cares what happens to you a great deal…as long as it is all bad!"

Chapter Thirteen
ROOM AT THE INN

Fifteen minutes after the attempted ambush we had put some distance between us and the attack site. I made sure we weren't being followed then pulled to the side of the road to catch our breath.

"We are going into his literal lair," I tried to make it is as clear as possible, "meaning your husband has the advantage, Maria. Are you still sure you want to go through with this? Is facing him and showing up at this meeting that important?"

She shuddered. "Yes!" she snapped. "And I hate when you call him 'my husband.'"

"Well, he is at the moment. But we have to play it cool; as if we did not connect him to the attacks because as much as it looks like he is deep in the middle of it all we have no proof. And we had better be as casual as we can be in front of him or anyone else. If there is a chance we can get out of this with no more violence and get you to a safe place we have to try to work it that way. And as to playing casual, we should if no other reason then that is could prejudice your case if it was known we were…intimate."

"I realize that, but it will be hard; even after these two days of, well, of controlling ourselves…" She gave a little laugh. "At least I could hug you and really only feel secure when you're holding me." She leaned over to me and we embraced. It was at the edge of passion, but I could not allow myself to be swept up.

"*Stay professional.*" I kept hearing my mother's voice which was always a wet blanket, though now a welcome one.

"You going to be okay?" I asked when we parted again.

"Yes," she sat up adjusting her hair. "As long as I know you're there, nearby, I can do this."

"We can do this," I corrected. "I'm with you every step of the way, kiddo."

•••

"There's the entrance!" Maria pointed as we rounded a long curve and came in sight of the stone posts of the gateway for our destination. The heavy wrought iron gate looked like something out of a European castle with bars a full two inches around. On a weathered board atop the posts were carved the words "The Lair—Keep Out."

"Well, at least he left a light on for strangers."

Maria flashed her smile at a carved three-headed dog on the gatepost that I could see had a camera in its open mouth of the center head.

"Cerberus as a security monitor." I grimaced. "At least he has a classical sense of humor."

"William bought this place almost the moment he got his first million," Maria explained. "It was like he had been waiting to live this lifestyle all his life…even though there was no indication of it when I first met him. Like he decided to be Charles Foster Kane the second he could afford to be."

The ornate gate slid noiselessly open liked the maw of a hungry beast ready to swallow us with a mechanical and modern smooth movement that belied its ancient look. I inched the car forward and as soon as we were within the space the gate closed behind us.

I suddenly felt a little chill as if someone had walked over my grave. I shook my head to vanish the image; last thing I needed was to jinx myself. One of the truisms of any battle, individual or collective is that it is won in the mind before the fight and I had to keep myself open to win even if I expected to lose.

The empty mind, the No-mind or *mushin* is part of my family heritage, practiced by Yagyu swordmasters for generations. "The mind must always be in the state of 'flowing,' for when it stops anywhere that means the flow is interrupted, in the case of the swordsman, it means death. Move with the mind, in order to move with the body" is one of the central tenets of the school.

I tried to keep my mind empty I drove up the long, tree-lined drive but the fact that I was heading into my enemy's home base with very little actual intelligence as to what I would face made that difficult.

Maria didn't help me keep an empty mind as she gave me a running commentary on the estate. "This place was built for a bootlegging king back during prohibition, his own personal castle that gave him a view across the river to Canada and more to the point, the cliffs below have caves in them that gave him a way to smuggle booze in directly from the river."

"Seems appropriate for some of the shady dealings that are rumored to swirl around William," I said. "But I do feel like I'm bringing Rapunzel into the tower instead of getting her out."

"I think it is more beauty and the beast," she gave me a light punch on my shoulder.

"And you would be which one?"

She punched me harder and laughed. It was good to break the tension of the last half hour. I had doubted she could handle the trip but now I thought she'd get through it okay. I just had to stay professional.

We rounded a copse of trees to come out onto a wide lawn and the spectacular and eerie house beyond came into full view. It was a squat, stark, Victorian beast painted in dark greens and purples that was set on an outcropping of granite very much like a medieval castle.

The mansion overlooked the St. Lawrence River from the edge of a high cliff. There were six turrets on the three-story structure and my first impression of it was that it reminded me of some gargoyle clinging to the rock face ready to pounce. As a security guy all I could think was that there were a hell of a lot of windows visible and a lot of space masked by greenery around the building. Lots of ways to get in, but that also meant a lot of ways to get out—that was good.

"Wow," I said. "Did he steal this place from the Addams Family, Morticia?" I got a smack on my arm from Maria for that.

"Be serious, Jon. He spent almost a year fitting the place out with tech; putting in its own private generator in a cavern below and a whole solar power array on the other side of that hill so he's completely off the grid and self-sufficient."

"I guess every king has to have his castle."

"More like an emperor his empire," she said bitterly. "So be prepared to bow and scrape."

"*That's* not going to happen," I grinned. "I bow to my Master in the *school* and that is about it. Even if I wasn't a Shadows I was a Marine."

She shot me a suddenly frightened look. "You won't antagonize him, will you?"

"Not to worry," I assured her, seeing she had a deep fear of him that had been obviously growing for a long time. "I know you have to do the party before you want to serve him the papers so I'll play the game as long as possible. And despite all that has happened, the attack on Dae Hoon, the goons after us, even that car we can not put it directly in his lap so a judge would make book on it, but we know he is behind it so I'll be on full guard dog alert, don't worry."

She looked at me a bit frightened and I saw she had a sudden thought.

"Don't we have to report that shooting to the police? I shot that man even if it was your gun. He is dead. I killed him." There was a little fear creeping back in to her voice

"I've been thinking about that." I did my best to sound positive. "I will get rid of the gun at the first opportunity and there is nothing to connect us to a body found on a country road; remember the car was rented under a cover identity. I suspect those goons will take their buddy's body and get rid of it themselves to keep from drawing police scrutiny."

I saw her relax just a bit as I brought the car around the sweeping drive to the other side of the house. There were five other cars parked there beyond an old-style carriage porch. A large barn or stable building was about forty yards further along the cliff edge, off the rock outcropping itself.

"I guess we're here," she sighed as I parked the car. She started to collapse in on herself. I had to stop that.

"You can do this, Maria. You're still the spit and vinegar chic from Flatbush you were in college." That didn't seem to bolster her terribly much so I added, "And you know I'm here to back you up; and for whatever comes after. Whatever."

"I'll be fine." She took a deep breath and tried a smile. "In fact, I can't wait to see your costume."

That made *me* shudder a bit. She had made a point of telling me that one of the other 'conditions' of their gathering was that all the Phools and any guests they brought had to be in costume. She had shipped her costume ahead weeks ago so we didn't have to worry about finding some odds and ends in a secondhand shop.

As for me, I had threatened to back out of helping her, jokingly, since I hate costumes, but when she said it didn't have to be anything too elaborate I settled on wearing my *Ninjutsu shinobi shozoku*—my traditional dark grey stealth suit. It had a mask and hood so it would pass for a 'costume.' It had served me in that capacity before. It had been in the sealed identity packet in my car as I always assumed if I were on the run I'd want my 'working' clothes as well.

"I'll get the two bags," I said as she exited the car.

"Maria!" A booming voice from the mansion made me start and I whirled.

A great bear of a man with shaggy red hair and a full beard, dressed as a Viking, complete with historically-inaccurate horned helmet enveloped Maria in a hug and swept her off her feet.

My 'bodyguard' reaction almost kicked in and I tensed to jump at him but she yelled, "Maxim!" with a giggle. "You've gotten even bigger!"

"And you've gotten prettier!" The giant said as he set her down. She located enough cheek on his face under the beard to give him a warm friendly kiss.

"And you still lie like an angel," she laughed. When she saw his eyes flash past her she turned to introduce me. "This is Jon Shadows; we were actually at Columbia for our first two years then he...uh...left."

Big Red enveloped my hand in his and almost shook it off me with his power. "Nice to meet you," he said. "Maxim Rudolf. I transferred into C.U. junior year and got co-opted into the Phools when I saw this angel in the library."

"I was born a fool," I confessed. "At least my mom says it's my only natural talent."

"He thinks he's funny, Maxim," Maria said, "but really, he is a good guy. A friend."

My statement made the giant roar and he slapped me on the shoulder with excess jocularity. "If Maria says so, I'll believe it," he grabbed one of the bags from me and we three went back through the door he'd come from. "The others are in the parlor but these stairs will take us up to your rooms so you can change."

'Eric the Red' took us up a narrow wooden staircase that I assumed must have been servants' stairs when the house was built. They led to a wide second floor corridor that was richly carpeted and paneled with expensive teak and oak. Everywhere the age and opulence of the building was on display with rich woods and carved wainscoting.

"This is your room, Maria," Maxim said as he set the bags down in a bedroom that was bigger than my apartment in New York City. "We didn't know you were bringing a guest this year...I mean with..."

"It's okay, Maxim. Jon knows the score...and will have his own room. I have no reason to antagonize William." She looked over at me with veiled eyes. "How is he?" She asked the faux Viking with trepidation. "I mean... his mood?"

The big man gave a massive shrug. "It's hard to tell, you know. He...he is happy at the beginning of a sentence then...well..." He seemed truly uncomfortable trying to analyze his host. Finally he concluded, "You'll have to take his temperature yourself. The others will be glad you're here though, I know I am."

He walked to a small mirror by the door and said in his booming voice, "Jeeves, attention!"

"Here, Mister Rudolf." A soft, well-modulated voice came from a hidden speaker.

"There will be a guest of Mrs. Carter that requires a room, preferably nearby her room."

The mirror flashed as if a soft light were reflected into it then the voice intoned, "I will see to it that the Golden Room is ready to receive the guest. Will that do, Mister Rudolf?"

"Excellent," Maxim said then turned to smile at me with a knowing smile. "That's only across the hall two doors down."

"That will be good," Maria ignored his implied 'naughty' suggestion.

"Wow," I exclaimed, "I guess I shouldn't be surprised the place is straight out of a science fiction comic book, considering William is Lex Luthor."

"More the Empire Strikes Back with the Emperor," Maxim joked.

She looked at me and I saw she wanted to talk about the divorce subpoena but didn't want to say anything in front of her friend. She seemed to realize that and smiled.

"I'll leave you to freshen up and change, Maria," I said. "And do the same myself. How long?"

"I'll be ready to come out of my cocoon in about a half hour or forty-five minutes."

I could see she was a little shaky and needed some time alone and, frankly, so did I, to collect my thoughts and make some plans.

"I'll knock then. We'll go down together."

Maxim hugged her again and was surprisingly quiet and gentle when he said, "It really is good to see you, hon. The place is just a big mausoleum without you here. I know the others really will be delighted to see you again too."

He grabbed my bag before I could and led me out of the room.

I looked back at Maria and shrugged. "It'll be fine; just a party until we have to leave, okay?" That got a wider smile back from her and I felt better about leaving her.

Chapter Fourteen
PARTY GAMES

"You can see why they call this the Golden Room," my Viking guide said when he dumped my bags on the bed of the room the computer had chosen for me.

The bedroom was aptly named with gold flocked wallpaper and all the furniture with a bronze or golden finish. Even the complex carved wood-work along the wall and on the massive headboard of the bed had a bur-nished hue to it.

I hope this isn't a yellow peril pun, I thought. I grinned at Maxim. "Wow it's like a room out of Goldfinger's bordello."

This caused the redhead to roar with laughter. "You're a card." Then his thick eyebrows knit and he leaned in and spoke in the closest to a whisper he could. "Is Maria okay? I know I haven't seen her in a year, but she seems really tense, even considering all the stuff with William, the estrangement and all."

"Just the long trip up," I tried to deflect any suspicions. "She'll be fine after she's had a shower." The last thing we needed was any hint she was going to serve Carter with papers. Their separation was an open secret but no one had any idea she was going to formally divorce him since both she and William were strict Catholics.

She had told me she would never wed again (I never believe *that* when someone says it) since she was Catholic, but that she could not in good conscience keep him 'chained' to her. And frankly, I think she felt a formal separation was not far enough from old William. I didn't even let myself speculate about a future she might have that might include me.

Stay professional!

"I'll bet you can use some rest as well," Maxim accepted my explana-tion. "I'll leave you to it; it is good to know Maria has...a friend right now, she...uh, needs it. She knows where we'll be when you're both dressed. See you later." He started to leave but stopped at the door and pointed to a gilt mirror beside it as an afterthought. "This is the access portal to Jeeves, you just have to say his name and he'll scan you and answer any questions you have." He waved and I was alone.

Well, mostly.

I stared at the mirror and felt the hairs on the back of my neck stand up. *Oh, I'm gonna be good and paranoid by the time this one is over with a robot brain watching my every move*, I thought. *Like I'm not already.*

I unpacked and showered with a constant creepy sense that I was under observation all the time; it was a disturbing feeling.

Don't let it freak you out, Jon; it's just like a mall, cameras everywhere to keep the shoplifters under control.

I was circumspect about my pistol while unpacking and kept it out of sight while I concentrated on donning my ninja uniform. I did my best to put Big Brother Jeeves out of my mind.

The name Ninjutsu means 'way of stealth' so I had the instinct to distrust surveillance in every fiber of my being. The chills kept running up and down my spine the whole time I was dressing.

Now, because of Maria again I was thinking hard about what it was I did. Sammo was dead because of my taking on a 'job'—that it was Maria was in many ways irrelevant—I had a hard time getting over that. It had cost me a marriage because of my newfound zeal to be available to those who needed me. And I suppose also by involving myself with other people's problems it was easier to gloss over my own.

Now, however I had to face what might have been the root of some of my own issues.

Damn, I wish you were here to talk to about this, Dae Hoon.

"Well, this turned into a real crap fest, Cuz," Sammo had said to me as we were crouched down behind a wall in an alley in Singapore two years before. He had pulled my ass out of a kidnap recovery operation that I had been hired for when it went bad. The local drug lord didn't like me cutting into his side business and his boys jumped me after I got her out. I spent a week as that lord's 'guest' and was in bad shape when Sammo came in guns blazing and got me out.

Bullets were chewing up the wood all around us. "I swear I don't know how you talk me into these jobs."

"Talk you into them?" I snapped off a few shots back at our adversaries. My vision wasn't too good as my left eye was swollen shut, but I just sprayed lead and hoped. "I don't remember even calling you; not that I'm complaining but you can't tell me you were 'just in the neighborhood.'"

"Okay, that's true," Sammo lobbed another shot at our pursuers. "I was lazing around my porch when Aunt Ondine called me."

"My mom called you?"

"Seems she heard from one of her old CIA contacts what you were doing and what had happened and they had no one who could do anything since it was, strictly a 'private matter.' So she sent me."

"And, mind you," I said as I reloaded the M16 I had 'acquired' from a guard who would have no use for it anymore. "I am thankful, but really surprised she bothered."

"Come again?" He pulled a hand grenade out of his flak vest and tossed it back. "She is your mother, last time I checked." The flash of the explosion was followed by a scream and moan.

"Well, yes," I said though I am sure my words were slurred by my swollen lips and broken teeth. "But when I decided to muster out of the Corps and to pick up dad's legacy she was not that supportive. Said I couldn't do it like dad, the usual." I was getting a bit dizzy but threw lead back at the garage I had been held in.

"Oh, come on, Cuz," he said, "You know she just misses him. You were a big disappointment to him when you didn't choose to follow his footsteps and all…"

"But then I did."

"But still she is angry you didn't decide to do it when he was alive, with that little side trip with that Italian girl and all."

"I never thought of it that way." I had to change clips on the Armalite. "But still doesn't explain why Mom called you?"

"Cause she didn't want her son dead, you dummy."

"Not because she thought I was a failure?" I didn't mean to sound as bitter as I did, but I wasn't at my best after a week of beatings.

"Of course not. When she called me she was upset I hadn't come in to back you up in the first place. She said *'You two are team like Anton and I used to be. He should have known better than to try it alone. He is good, but everyone needs backup.'*"

"She said that?"

"Yes."

"Damn. I guess I'm gonna have to call you for most of my sneak jobs then."

"See," he said with fake disgust, "I was afraid you'd get me involved in more of your shenanigans if I told you the truth."

"So why didn't you lie, I mean you're a ninja."

"But I also was a Boy Scout."

"There it is then. I guess I'm stuck with you."

"Yup!"

"Let's kill the rest of these sons-of-bitches. I'm dying for a real meal and a hot bath."

"Might want to see a dentist before you eat much," he pointed out.

"Shut up and keep shooting. And pass me a hand grenade."

He had backed me up on any job that was more than a one-man job after that and never failed me. I was going to miss Sammo every freaking day.

How the hell am I gonna get by without you, Cuz?

Chapter Fifteen
PARTY TIME!

I stood in the 'golden room' and took a deep breath. Dwelling on Sammo was not going to do me any good; the reality was that Maria was the live client and it was her that I had to focus on taking care of. That and getting ready for the costumed ball where I was going to meet this ogre out of nightmares, William Carter. That was the action of the moment.

My 'costume' was the 'stealth suit' I always traveled with, my own modern variation on the traditional *Ninpo* garb. It was dark charcoal grey, not black like in the movies (because black actually stands out at night, whereas dark grey blends in) and wrapped across the front exactly like a karate *gi* except with a bunch of hidden pockets. I found it actually more comfortable than my Corps uniform for much of what I did. There was a separate, two-piece hood that was better than a Balaclava and, for purposes of the party made it look like a 'costume.'

Of course, it was not a costume to me, but it would be spectacular enough to the crowd below and I wouldn't feel out of place—I had worn some form of uniform most of my life and this particular one was very much as comfortable as the pajamas most people thought of them as. My customization on my version had a sewn-in holster for my Glock that I slipped comfortably in under my arm, its weight very reassuring.

I looked in the mirror when I was ready to head over to Maria's and had to smile; I looked to me like I was ready to head out to teach *a ninjutsu* class on any normal day—the thought of going to a party in my 'work clothes' tickled my sense of irony. But looking into the mirror also made me think of the circuitry behind it. I had forgotten for a moment that I was probably under surveillance.

"Jeeves?" I said.

"Yes, sir?" the same neutral voice replied. "I do not recognize you; could you identify yourself, please?"

"Jonathan Shadows." I started to put on the hood then realized I had better hold off.

"Hold still for a moment while I record your features, sir." There was a briefest pause and then the voice said, "Jonathan Shadows of Union City, New Jersey, United States of America?"

"That's the one." *Wow, with Google Earth and all that, there really is not*

"My mom called you?"

gonna be much use for a P.I. pretty soon.

"I shall attempt to anticipate your needs, sir. How can I help you at this time?"

"Uh, could you tell me if Mrs. Carter is out of the shower?"

"The lady is fully dressed and awaiting your return."

"Okay," I had a little chill with the A.I. having that sort of information, but then realized I might be able to use it so I pressed. "Can you tell me where Mister Carter is?"

"I am afraid that information is restricted, sir. Is there some other way I can assist you?"

So, the puppet master does have something to hide.

"Thank you, Jeeves, that will be all for the moment."

I went out across to Maria's room and knocked on the door. "It's Jon, you ready to go?"

Instead of answering the door opened and there, standing tall and looking regal was Maria as Marie Antoinette! Her dress was peach-colored and covered with lace and embellishments that made her look like she had stepped off the top of a wedding cake.

Her raven hair was concealed under an elaborate white, powdered wig and her dusky completion was powdered down to porcelain doll tones complete with a beauty mark on her left cheek.

"What do you think, Bruce Lee?" she asked.

"More like Sho Kosugi," I corrected with a chuckle then added, "How the hell did you do all that in a half hour?"

"Forty-one minutes, actually," she corrected as she stepped from the room to hold out her hand in a queenly gesture for me to grasp. "But who's keeping track?"

"No one, obviously." I took her hand and escorted her down the hallway. The *Sulsa-Do* of my father's style had, in days of old, been both bodyguards and spies for the Korean courts and on her arm I felt like one of the real old *Hwa Rang* warriors doing bodyguard duty on a noblewoman. "Now I know why you shipped it all ahead. You would have needed a small truck to hold all the suitcases for this."

"Only a fraction of what I had in them, Jon," she giggled. "But I really do travel light most of the time, as you saw; not nearly the high maintenance creature I used to be. I just draw the line at thrift store underwear."

She took the lead directing me to the top of a classically wide grand staircase. There she stopped suddenly and turned to me, her face paler under the make up. "Jon, I'm scared."

"Easy, kiddo," I assured her, "try to think of this as exactly like any other time you've had this little get together. We won't serve him until the end so there is nothing to worry about; and he will not dare do anything drastic in his own home with everyone here as witnesses. You have to realize he tried so hard to keep you from here for that very reason."

Her painted face brightened and she took a deep breath. "Okay, then. We're ready to go."

"Just one thing."

"Yes?"

"Don't lose your head, Marie, Madame La Farge is a bitch!"

It took her a second, but when she got it she laughed so hard she almost fell off her platform shoes.

That's how we made our royal entrance into the party below, laughing like two half-wits and I knew she would be alright.

The ballroom of the mansion was done up in grand Victorian style but with twenty-first century twists. There was a massive crystal chandelier hanging over the center of the vaulted space, flashing different colored lights in an almost hypnotic pattern in what I was sure was a programmed sequence. The floor was oak parquet with one wall consisting of full-length windows that showed a view out over the water to Canada on the other side of the St. Lawrence.

The wall opposite the windows was the real twist; it was a floor-to-ceiling LCD display that showed a full orchestra playing swing music from some other location. I later learned that it was a live digital feed from a studio in Buffalo. It was eerie for it felt like they were just on the other side of a glass wall till you tilted your head one way or the other.

The Phirewall Phools were all in attendance in full costume, standing at the buffet tables against the far wall with drinks in their hands and looking vaguely uncomfortable, like kids at the eighth grade dance, not sure what to do. As we walked down the staircase to the room there was a long frozen second before they noticed us.

Maria gave me a quick scorecard as we walked across the room to meet them: "The pale-looking pirate is Harvey Walters and on his arm, the even paler Lindsey Lohan look-alike is Andrea Stein. You met Maxim and that very tiny Peter Pan beside him is Johanna Antar—they have been going together since college like me and William—only somehow they managed to keep it alive and fresh and working." She choked up on that but continued the whispered, guided tour. "The gaudy cowboy and the overly made-up Indian are Mike Cudney and Ian Holter and yes, they are a couple. And hard body Batgirl who looks like a personal trainer is Susie Smith; she lost her husband to cancer last year."

"They look less nerdy than I thought a gathering like this would," I said. When she arched an eyebrow at me in disdain I added, "Mind you, still looks like the waiting area at ComicCon, but they mostly look like healthy thirty-somethings."

"All things considered in this society, they have enough money to stay healthy," she said with a sour smile. "At least on the outside; I'm not so sure about some of their insides."

"But I don't see the puppet master himself. I would think he'd be holding court like the proverbial head cock in the hen house."

Her pretty face screwed up to match her sour tone. "His sense of drama will make him want to have the grand entrance."

"This from Marie Antoinette?"

She stuck out her tongue.

The group all seemed to notice us at once and turned to stare in a pregnant moment that hung suspended in the air like smoke from a forest fire.

"Maria!" Peter Pan/Johanna in her green tights festooned with leaves and wearing a little pointy hat, flitted across the room. The little faux-fae and the French queen embraced with great joy. That seemed to put the others in motion and they all swarmed my friend and the ice was broken. Suddenly it was a group of magpies chattering away.

It was amazing to feel the abrupt change in the tone of the room and wonderful to see any residual tension in Maria washed away by the wave of hugs. She and her friends talked, catching up on the last year a mile-a-minute.

It was funny to me, thinking that they would be internet connected so it shouldn't be that much to catch up on, but from the sound of them, most had drifted apart in the last decade as so many people do and just did the 'holiday' emails. Somehow, the personal touch made the difference and they were all doing emotional time traveling together.

It made me realize all the more how much I would miss Sammo as time went on, and made me conscious of how much an outsider I was with this group.

It could only get more interesting from that point out.

Chapter Sixteen
BEHIND THE MASKS

I was introduced all around to the menagerie of Phools and had a little surprise; it turned out that Ian Holter, dressed as the Indian from the Village People, actually remembered me from freshman year at Columbia!

I had absolutely no memory of him, but that's not surprising since I had lost a couple of years to an alcoholic haze and frankly, I wasn't sure his actually remembering me was all that good. I was a dick back then. Still, it made my attendance completely plausible and deflected any suspicion that I was anything like a bodyguard or process server and didn't belong.

The general attitude seemed to be they were happy to see Maria with someone who actually cared about her, though no one made any off-color jokes; they were just as happy if I *were* just an old friend. I felt like these people really did care for each other like family, albeit distantly.

For about thirty or so minutes everybody chatted, hugged, laughed and caught up. I did my best deflecting questions about what I really did for a living—with 'corporate litigation' (I was licensed for the bar in New York and New Jersey) being vague enough to cover my dubious background.

They all seemed an amiable group and I found myself warming to them, and was especially happy to see Maria so at ease with the group. It was like looking back in time to when she was happy and hopeful; I only hoped it was a glimpse of the future as well.

Suddenly the room lights began to dim and the live feed band stopped playing the song they were jamming on. Everyone sort of looked around and held their breath as the chandelier's light splintered into shards of red and purple.

Everyone became unnaturally quiet. It was eerie but I found a chill of expectation at what would come next, as I imagined everyone else did. We weren't disappointed.

A Bach *cantata* seemed to flow out of the walls all around us, growing in volume to fill the room till the sound pressed against our guts like a cold embrace. Then a hidden panel in the LCD screen slid up and there, dressed in the skull-faced visage of The Red Death from the silent film version of *The Phantom of the Opera* was our host, William Carter!

The ballroom was dead quiet as the skull-faced image of the Phantom came through the center of the LCD screen. He wore a scarlet robe and plumed hat like Lon Chaney had in the motion picture but instead of the full-face skull the actor had worn in the old silent, he had the half mask more like the Broadway musical. He had a walking stick and he moved theatrically across the dance floor with an arrogant strut.

"Good evening, my friends," the macabre figure said. His voice was raspy as if he was straining to speak. "It is good to see that all of you Phools could grace my home once more."

I was as fascinated by the reactions of the other Phirewall Phools to our host as with Carter himself. There seemed to be a general distaste for the new arrival all around and maybe even a little fear in the faces of some of the assembled group of long-time friends.

Maria stiffened and shuddered a bit and took hold of my arm at the elbow. When I looked over at her I realized she looked terrified!

"Easy, Maria," I whispered. "He can't harm you and he will know nothing of the papers till we are on the way out. It's just like any other meeting; hold onto that thought and you can get through this." She seemed to take courage then and brightened up a bit.

"So good to see you all," the raspy phantom said with an expansive sweep of his arms. "But especially my queen, the most lovely Marie Antoinette." He glided toward her with an almost unnatural smoothness till he stood a little more than arm's length from the two of us.

Close up, William Carter was every bit as frightening as the character he was dressed as. Despite the white make-up on the exposed part of his face I could see there was scar tissue peeking out from the edges of the Phantom of the Opera half-mask. Whatever had happened to him in the rest of his body, his face had taken a good part of the punishment in the accident. Maria had not really prepared me for the extent of it.

"You are looking well, dear wife," Carter rasped. He leaned in to give Maria a peck on the cheek and she worked to suppress a shudder but did nothing to stop him. She even gamely smiled. "Are you not going to introduce your old friend, darling?"

"I'm sorry, William, it was a very long drive." Maria stammered, "This is Jon Shadows. You may have heard me talk about him before—"

"Columbia, wasn't it?" William asked. He extended his hand to take mine and his grip was surprisingly firm, though his flesh was cold. "What year did you graduate?"

"I didn't," I answered with a smile. "I matriculated to the school of hard knocks and finally got my degree while in the Marines."

The garishly costumed Carter gave a cold smile. His eyes were bright violet with the pupils tiny and isolated in fields of white. He stared at me with an almost reptilian intensity.

"Very nice you could come to our little soiree," Carter said. "We shall endeavor to show you the best of times." After his 'greeting' he turned away as a royal dismissal and faced the rest of the guests.

"Okay, fellow Phools," he rasped. "I know I have not been able to attend the last two meetings because of my…uh…inability to drive while filled to the brim with cheap whiskey." This admission to fallibility from the outrageous figure brought a few nervous laughs from the group but most seemed mesmerized by his performance. It had me wondering what was coming next as I tried to figure out exactly who and what the man behind the mask was.

"I am gratified that you all agreed to let me attend the other meetings via teleconference," he continued. "And to have you all in my home is a very special treat for me, as I don't often have drop-in visitors." Now he laughed softly, though in context of his outfit what might have been a gentle laugh had a sinister lilt.

"Very much a treat indeed!" He continued, "I know I have been remiss in communicating these last few months but I promise you I have had a reason that is both sound and exciting!" He turned and with a wave of his walking stick at the LCD screen caused the now complete wall of images to become an enlarged image of his face on a live feed from cameras somewhere in the room.

"When I lay at death's door I had a vision." He turned to face the crowd, his tone now almost a revival preacher's harangue. "I realized that we had been all wrong; we had spent all our time trying to reinvent the wheel by staring into the void of the future. Instead of always trying to do the newest and best we should have been looking backward; look back to the secrets that the ancients knew. I have spent the last year in intense research, my friends. And what I have discovered in these studies will revolutionize the world as we know it."

He whirled to face us all with arms upraised as if conjuring and the giant image of his face gave the whole scenario a horrific and bizarre tone.

It was strange to see him there, live, and his face twenty times larger than life behind him covering the entire wall. In that image he looked truly demonic, the evil light in his eyes almost shining with a twisted internal light. I was irrationally very glad for my Glock in the holster inside my jacket.

"Many of you will think me brash or misguided," a ghost of smile flickered across his thin lips. "But if you think about what I am going to tell you, you should first think about the fact that the first lasers were generated through crystals, and as you know we are now using crystals to store terabytes of data."

"We know all that, William," Cowboy Mike Cudney said with a sneer. "Crystal technology is the future for much of the computing world—"

"And the past, Mikey boy, and the past!" Carter countered, "That is the truth of it." His giant image regarded the Phools with a new distain. "I have rediscovered techniques, very secret techniques that were long lost to the world. I might even say 'legendary techniques." He laughed and I swear it was tinged with not a little bit of madness.

"As legend would have it," he proclaimed, "well over 11,000 years ago there existed an island nation in the middle of the Atlantic Ocean. This great nation was populated by a noble and powerful race of people who were veritable techno-magicians. This amazing place, this golden paradise was called by a Greek philosopher 'Atlantis' and is believed to have flourished from about 60,000 to 11,000 BCE. I have rediscovered their most amazing secrets!"

Chapter Seventeen
ISLAND DREAMS

Everyone in the room stared at this grotesque figure of William Carter with stunned expressions and several even gasped as his brazen pronouncement. For a long moment no one said a word then both Johanna Antar/Peter Pan burst out laughing.

The laughter made Carter snap his head around so quickly that his hat flew off as he snarled at her. "Do not laugh at me! You need to hear, to understand!" The woman choked her laugh off and her eyes went wide with a sudden and new fear at his dark, threatening tone.

"The people of this island we call Atlantis," the skull masked genius rambled on, "possessed great wealth thanks to their island's natural resources. Atlantis was a center for trade and commerce with colonies all over the world—which, by the way, explains the similarities of so many cultures— pyramids the world over and language similarities and so on. But they also had a Great Crystal. It was called the "*Tuaoi* Stone" and it is said it was a huge cylindrical prism that was used to gather and focus energy from the cosmos. This crystal allowed the Atlanteans to do all kinds of fantastic things, or so the legends say."

He was on a roll now, his voice crackling with energy that was reflected in his wild gestures as he spoke, his arms sweeping in gestures to point at a map of the legendary island that appeared on the screens behind him like a demonic Powerpoint lecture.

"They could change the form of living things and actually transmute matter." He continued, "It was a virtually limitless source of power. But these people of the island nation got greedy and stupid, tuned up their crystal to too high a frequency and set off volcanic disturbances that led to the destruction of their whole world."

Carter did a pirouette like a stage magician and giggled as his image filled the LCD screen again. "Yes, they got it wrong and I…I got it right. I figured out the puzzle. I know the vibration code to it all; I have the sonic key!"

"Are you saying you have found Atlantis?" Maxim Rudolf asked with no attempt to hide his amusement. "That sort of fairy tale—"

"They laughed at Heinrich Schliemann," Carter snapped, "when they said the legends of Troy were just that…legends…fanciful stories! But he was proven to be right and he discovered, uncovered Troy and it was proven to be real." He laughed that strange cackling laugh again and I knew I was in the presence of someone who was not wrapped too tight. "But…no I have not found that great lost island-continent. No, my discovery is something that even skeptics like yourself will have to admit is true and real. I have, by researching ancient documents and by trial and error duplicated the Tuaoi Stone and its amazing powers."

The Phools now muttered among themselves, still stunned by his strange announcement and his reaction to Maxim's challenge to it. None wanted to invoke his wrath but finally Maria spoke up.

"William," she said in a steady voice that I knew was forced. I was proud of her for standing up. "Are you saying that you have found the harmonic frequencies that allow for the transmutation of matter…that is, in other words, you have found the Philosophers' Stone?"

"Yes!" Carter exclaimed. "Give that woman a cigar! You see, you see all of you why I married that woman in the first place? She gets it. Yes, by golly, she sure as hell gets it. Yes; I have decoded the secret of transmutation of matter."

"But that sort of atomic change can only be achieved in a super collider," Maria said. "That alchemical stuff is—"

"Don't you dare say it," Carter screamed, his hoarse voice cracking. "Your narrow minds could not see the possibilities of Facebook or the Phools Phorum and now, now you are in the same line with those nay-sayers who laughed at Tesla."

"William—" Maria began but I shot her a look because I could see something in his eyes that I had seen before in Fallujah and a dozen places since; Old William really had gone completely around the bend! It would not take much to send him into violence, I could see now why she had feared coming to confront him.

"No, dear wife," Carter said. "I knew there would be doubts about my discoveries…I mean Galileo, Gates, all the greats were doubted, but I can deal with that." He glided over to Maria and reached out to touch the back of the knuckles of his right hand to her cheek. She gave a little shudder.

"I only ask that all of you have an open mind about it," Carter said with a soft laugh, apparently not noticing his wife cringe. "I will tell you more later, but let us enjoy this gathering of found family." He snapped his fingers and the band on the virtual screen began to play again, this time some soft dance music.

Everyone looked around confused for a second, not making a move as the popular music of twenty years ago filled the room and started to echo off the walls. After a few moments Batgirl Susie walked up to Viking Maxim and grabbed him by the arm to pull him onto the dance floor. That broke the ice for the rest and they began to wander out to the floor in a loose group. In a few bars everyone but Carter, Maria and I were dancing with an almost desperate abandon, as if the gyrations could shake off the demented ravings they had heard minutes before. They were longtime friends so couples and then groups of three began to dance together, switching partners or just dancing in clumps.

"Not dancing, Maria?" William asked. "You always loved to shake a leg."

She tried not to look over at me, but I saw the veiled terror in her eyes. "I don't know, William. This gown is…uh…." She indicated her wide pannier and shrugged.

"Oh, dear," Carter laughed, "not to worry, I'm not as spry as I used to be either." He swept forward and held out a hand to her and she reluctantly took it.

The bizarre image of the scarlet skull-faced man and the powder-white queen of France was almost enough to top the evening, and might have made me chuckle if I could not see the deep fear in her eyes as her husband slowly swept her away and whirled her around the floor.

As if on cue (and I suspect it was) the music switched to a slow dance and Carter pulled Maria to him. I felt a chill at it and a little bit of jealousy. That surprised me, as I thought I was beyond both at that moment.

I was then startled when a hand reached over to touch my arm. It was

Susie Smith, the Catwoman.

"No wallflowers here," she held out her arms to me. I couldn't really refuse without looking like the bodyguard I was supposed to be, so I stepped over to her and let her put her arms around me.

She was about a foot shorter than me and thin, but in shape so when I put my arm around her in return, I felt muscle. She had a dancer's form and fit nicely into me so that we moved out onto the dance floor smoothly.

"Don't worry if you can't dance," she purred with a sultry voice. She looked up at me with wide hazel eyes and a sly smile. "I'm sure I can help you move right, at least you could if you put your mind to it."

Like most martial artists, actually I *could* dance, as a lot of traditional schools—like both of those of my parents—required black belt candidates to play a musical instrument or perform a traditional dance. The idea was that most combat really had a rhythmic component. I had also been forced to take ballroom classes by my mom in high school, and soon discovered it was a great way to pick up girls, so got enthusiastic about it.

Now, however, my mind was on Maria dancing a dozen feet away with William. I could see she was stiff but working at a smile and holding up under the press of her skeletal husband.

"So how well do you know Maria?" Susie asked. She made the most of pressing her well-exercised form against me as we swayed to the slow music. "I mean, she never mentioned you before to me, that I know of."

I did my best to be pleasant at the intrusive inquiry. "We dated back in college," I said as noncommittally as I could. "And with the glory of the internet we reconnected a little while ago."

"Reconnected?" She spoke with as much innuendo as she could put in it.

"It was a long drive up. She wanted company, you know, someone to talk to."

"Company is important," Susie smiled suggestively. "I often could use someone to uh...talk to." I was suddenly too aware of her body pressing into me when it did not have to while we danced.

Here I was stuck on the horns of a dilemma; I was head over heels with Maria yet trying to make it seem casual for the benefit of the crowd and her megalomaniac husband. Now I was being straight-up propositioned by a horny widow who was clearly a woman who was used to getting any man she set her claws for. And she most certainly would cry wolf if I turned her down. Not a situation one could train for in the *dojang*.

I swayed to the music with her while simultaneously attempting to not be her scratching post and tried to think of a gentlemanly way to turn her down without blowing my cover.

Then my 'salvation' came in from most unexpected source in the form of a sudden shriek from William Carter himself!

Chapter Eighteen
CRYSTAL CLEAR AT LAST

"Don't 'William' me, Maria," the skull-faced host yelled as he suddenly pushed Maria away from him almost violently. "You don't tell me you are not ready to be with me again and say it has nothing to do with the way I look. Don't you think I know who that damned hired hand is at your side? Nothing but a half-breed stallion brought to service a rutting mare!"

He waved a hand and suddenly the wall-to-ceiling screen showed me and Maria talking in the hallway upstairs. Our whole conversation was played out in garish excess on the big screen;

"Jon, I'm scared."

"Easy, kiddo," I said, *"try to think of this as exactly like any other time you've had this little get together. We won't serve him until the end so there is nothing to worry about."*

"You think I would let you divorce me, Maria?" Carter screamed. "To take my wealth and ruin me after you have sucked the life out of me all these years? Not so fast, Maria. Not so fast! And it is fitting you are trying insinuate yourself with these turncoat bastards as well, since they have been leeching off me for decades!"

The dance music stopped.

The Phools were beyond confused now and each shot looks all around and it was clear they were scared of the wild outburst. They looked over at me with accusing eyes, with even Susie stepping away to look up at me with new eyes.

I walked swiftly across the dance floor to directly face Carter, stepping partially between him and Maria. There was no need for stealth now, no subterfuge or obfuscation needed. Better to get it over with while there were all the witnesses available in one room.

"William Jonas Carter," I said in a loud voice, "Before these witnesses I officially serve you with these articles of divorce." I took the papers from a pocket in my *gi* and thrust them at him, jamming them into his out-stretched hand.

The garish crimson figure looked at the papers in his bony hand and began to vibrate with rage. He tossed the papers back at me with a snarl.

"You vermin!" he yelled. "How dare a lowlife creature like you have the nerve to accost me in my own home! Me, William Carter the great!"

Maria backed away from Carter and pressed against my back, keeping her eyes fixed on her husband.

"William," she said. "Don't do this. Let me go, please for what we were."

"To cuckold me with that half-breed welp?" He screamed, "and to make fun of me with these witless morons here?"

The Phools were getting angry and some started to move forward at the red-clad host.

"There's no need to use that kind of inflammatory language, William—" Ian Holter, dressed as the Indian said in a strained voice. He walked toward Carter with his hands up in a pleading gesture.

Carter whirled and thrust the walking stick at the faux redman. The stick had a crystal top piece I hadn't noticed before and when he touched the chest of the approaching 'Indian,' a bolt of electrical energy leapt from it.

Holter was lifted off his feet and propelled backward with a shriek as the force of the electrical discharge slammed him to the floor.

Several of the women yelled and Holter's lover, Cudney, ran to Holter's side to cradle the fallen man in his arms.

"Are you out of your mind, William?" Maria yelled. She started to head for her husband, more angry than scared, but I grabbed her before she got in range of his 'zap stick.'

William was in full form now, his raspy vice raised in volume as he exhorted all of us. "You will all know how wrong you were to turn your backs on me when this day is done." He backed away from us and laughed. He waved his wand and suddenly the light from the windows was gone as steel shutters slammed down to seal the portals off. There were sounds from deeper in the house that I knew were other windows being sealed in the same fashion. "Especially you, my dear Jezebel of a wife and your half-breed stud."

Now I moved for him, aware that he was trapping us in the building and that was something I had to try to stop.

He saw me coming and I was sure he was going to level the giant taser at me but instead two masked men, from their build the same two that had survived our dustup on the road, came out of a concealed panel behind Carter. Both of the men had miniature versions of their leader's stun-stick held menacingly in one hand, and *tanto* knives in the other.

I turned to confront the two men who came straight at me, but Carter used the distraction to grab Maria.

Before I could react to her scream of "help me" Maria and Carter vanished back through the panel the goons had come from.

The two men were still masked but they came at me with *tanto*-style knives this time, not just their taser billy-clubs and it was clear they intended to gut me. I guess my popularity with the Japanese goon set had dropped to a record low.

I stepped back to receive the first attacker with an open-handed slap at the lunging blade. It was a clumsy lunge. The *tanto* is not the weapon to lunge with effectively so it turned into a slash that almost took off my lead arm. He swiped at me with the taser stick but I dodged that as I drew my pistol and shot the son of the rising sun right in the face. You can wear a bullet-resistant vest, but you can't armor your face.

Several of the women, Susie included, screamed.

I spun to draw down on the second attacker but goon number two screamed like a Girl Scout on fire and turned to head back through the panel he had come from.

He was out of luck, however, because his boss had closed the door the second he and his prisoner were through it. The masked man began to yell and pound on it.

It was a pathetic sight!

My mother was right, you just can't get good assassins anymore.

I re-holstered my gun and grabbed a nearby chair that I broke over the whiner's back to knock him out.

"I will make you pay." The giant image of the grinning skull-faced Carter said from the LCD wall. He was holding a squirming and terrified looking Maria. "All of you, for ignoring me, 'humoring me' when I know I have found the true answer to power. And for all of you deserting me when I was hurt. And you, Shadows, most of all I hate you for cuckolding and persecuting me! You think I don't know she was thinking of you even before my accident? She planned all this to humiliate me."

Maria's eyes seemed to stare directly and accusingly off the wall at me as if to scream, "*Some help you were, Jon.*"

I was proving to be a pretty lousy bodyguard! I had to fight the cold feeling in the center of my gut that I was going to lose her the way I had lost Sammo.

Stay professional!

"What the hell is going on?" Maxim Rudolf asked. The great bear of a

Holter was lifted off his feet…

man threw himself against the metal shutter that had slammed over the French windows while his Peter Pan wife stood at his side, looking terrified.

Other members of the group had moved to test each of the other windows and one, the Pirate, Harry Walters, ran to try the front door. No one had any luck.

"Sealed tight!" the Pirate observed pointlessly. "He had to have planned this for a long time." The fear in his voice was palpable and I have to admit I shared it. The whole scenario was like some diabolical plot from a horror movie.

"What kind of mind has all this stuff installed?" I asked aloud.

"You can't blame that on William, I'm afraid," Peter Pan said. The first shock of the situation had apparently worn off and she was breathing normally.

"How so?"

"This place was built during prohibition by a smuggler," Johanna/Peter Pan explained. "He literally built it like a fortress with these steel shutters and all. When William bought the place and had the wiring upgraded he had all the servos upgraded as well. He joked about it two years ago at the meeting via Skype. Said he had the place for us all to come if the zombie apocalypse ever actually happened."

"Great." I moved to the panel Carter had gone through while I tried to assess our options, my mind going a mile a minute. I was sure he had planned this, and must have had me watched from my first contact with Maria, maybe even before from what he said about suspecting her of infidelity.

I sure as hell was not going to blame some bootlegger for the customized insanity of The Lair. Not by a long shot; I had seen enough to know that William Carter was sick in mind as well as body and the setup was all part of some warped revenge scheme.

"We have to find a way to get out of here," the cowboy said with more than a little panic in his voice; his Indian companion was shakily on his feet now but still looking far too white for the role he played.

"We have to find William, get Maria and slap the stupid out of that idiot husband of hers," Maxim said.

"That is a sentiment I can get behind," I concurred. "But it is the how we do it that is really the issue here, isn't it?"

Chapter Nineteen
IN THE MAZE OF MADNESS

"**T**his all has to be some sort of horrible joke," Peter Pan said hopefully but then she glanced over at the bloody corpse of the yakuza thug that I had ventilated.

All this time the giant face of the ghastly genius loomed over us from the giant TV screen. It made me think of the old superstition about mirrors, how it was believed that it was through them that death entered rooms. It's why they used to cover mirrors in the homes of the newly dead. And that gave me an inspiration.

"Jeeves," I said aloud. "He's at all the doors and mirrors; we need to disable or destroy them to get any privacy." All the computer geniuses in the room and I'm the one who had to think of that.

Several members moved to the wall-set Jeeves in the corner of the room and then several of them simply smashed it with a chair. *Well, that is one way,* I thought. *So much for sophisticated minds.*

The big Viking pointed to a long medieval-type bench along one wall. "We should be able to use that as a battering ram. We might be able to take the shutters off; they had to have been originally built to keep people out, not in." He indicated to two others and they moved to pick up the bench. The three of them moved toward one of the shuttered windows with the heavy wooden bench.

"No," I said, "try the panel Carter went though. It's bound to be easier to smash and that is where Maria is."

Maxim nodded. "Yes, that makes sense."

They turned around and slammed the bench into the wall panel. The LCD cracked and shattered into a thousand glass shards to reveal the metal frame and laminated wood panel beneath. That gave way after only three hard hits, the glass and metal splintering to reveal a dark opening beyond.

We all stood for a moment with no one quite sure what to do next. This was not their world; it was very much mine. I grabbed the *tanto* from the fallen yakuza and said, "I'll go first." I held up my gun and gave a grim smile.

"I'll stay with this one," Peter Pan offered. She had the goon I'd beaned with the chair bound hand and foot and held a brass urn as a club. "Save Maria!"

"We'll go as well," the cowboy and his Indian volunteered as well. Maxim hugged his wife. "I'll be back as quick as I can be, Johanna," he assured her.

"You coming, Henry?" Maxim asked the pirate who in turn looked at his pale partner Andrea. She nodded and the two joined us.

Then we went into the opening.

The corridor behind the panel was narrow enough that Maxim could barely squeeze his pseudo-Norse mass through it behind me. There were red-tinted strip lights that made it easy to navigate but I still moved cautiously, alert for booby traps.

I found the first one twenty feet along in the narrow corridor. My instinct felt the open hall was a bit too easy, so I dropped to my knees and pulled some powder out of one of my stealth jacket pockets that I normally would use to blow into opponent's eyes to blind him and, using a short rubber blow gun, blew a low mist ahead of me. About three feet on the dust revealed an electric eye beam, faintly visible in the low, red light.

"If we can see one," I told to Max who was pressing right behind me, "Then there are three more; simple rule of thumb."

The question was, what did the beam do—was it just an alarm for someone in the hall or did it trigger some sort of trap?

I held up a hand and halted the four behind me.

"This was really well planned," I said. "And you gotta know by now that Carter is nuts, so this could be really bad from here on out."

"What do you mean?" Catwoman-Susie asked.

"I mean as bad as it gets; deadly. Might be better to wait while I go ahead; this is the kind of thing I do too damn often…not something you do."

"Just who are you?" The Viking asked.

"*What* are you?" Susie asked.

"Let's just say I do this sort of thing as a matter of course, professionally. So I am equipped to do this."

"It doesn't matter; Maria is our friend," the Viking said. "I'm gonna keep on."

"Yes," Susie put a hand on my arm. "We keep going." She wasn't letting competition trump friendship and I had to give it to her for that.

The Pirate and Lindsey Lohan look-alike agreed and the two of them nodded in unison. Maria had good friends; it made me proud she cared for me and all the more angry at that lunatic, her husband.

With the gang behind me I stepped forward and broke the eye-beam, holding my breath to see what would follow.

Nothing.

For a long moment nothing. We all took a collective deep breath and moved forward.

Then I heard it, a slight, whispered hiss.

"Down!" I called and ducked. The others followed and dropped as a line of darts flew at head-height over us to thud into the wall. They were not unlike pub darts in size and hit the wall hard enough to vibrate.

"Holy crap!" the Pirate yelled.

"Stay down," I ordered. "And don't touch any of the darts." My *Ninpo* mind went to the darts being probably covered with poison. If they were to be effective, I'd have at least coated them with a paralyzing agent, so I had to assume that my skull-faced opponent would do the same.

"He could have really hurt us," Susie said with a breathy hesitation. "I mean…seriously." She was obviously having a hard time adjusting her mind to the world of sudden death. Most people do who live in a civilized world.

"At the very least," I said. No reason to make them more paranoid, but the fact is that if the mad genius wanted to stop us pursuing him, darts with poison were the least of the things he could throw at us. Explosives, gas, electricity. It was all in the mix for the next booby trap.

The sane thing to do would be to back out and call a SWAT team. The corridors ahead were a pathway to hell; but Maria was ahead of me and I had no idea what that nutjob might do if I waited.

"Stay spread out," I directed, "and watch every step. Try to walk where I do."

I moved forward then on all fours, fingers and toes, my eyes everywhere. Ten feet further down the corridor turned sharply and I could see a seam in the floor just past the turn. It was slight, and if I had been walking instead of low to the floor I would not have seen the slight difference.

Once more I stopped everyone.

"I think it's a pressure plate," I whispered. "I need something heavy enough to set it off."

In a moment Harvey Walters, the pirate, tapped me on the leg and pointed to his high pirate boots.

"Yes," I nodded. "One of them should do it." He shucked off the boot and handed it to me. I hefted it and decided it should be enough. "Watch your eyes, I have no idea what will happen."

I checked to make sure everyone was ready then tossed the boot hard onto the suspect floor section.

This time the reaction was immediate and violent; a deafening explosion rocked the whole corridor with the sound of multiple impacts from shrapnel pinging off the walls.

"Damn!" I heard Maxim cry behind me, almost at my ear though he sounded a mile away. He started to move but I reached out to stop him.

"Stay down," I called loudly though my deafened ears only heard it as a faint murmur. "Sometimes they—"

As I spoke a second explosion went off, smaller than the first but with the same multiple pings all around. Dust was everywhere and for a long slice of time it seemed it would never settle, but gradually the haze cleared enough and I raised my head.

"Stay down," I yelled, then turned and mimed for everyone to stay down. I moved forward again slowly.

Where the floor had been was a long deep hole about six feet across. The walls were pockmarked with hundreds of tiny craters from what I assumed was ball-bearing shrapnel. There was nothing left of the boot at all.

That would have been us if we were impatient.

Ahead I could see a door that was slightly ajar with moonlight streaming in.

"Let's move," I said but didn't wait to see if they followed or not. I moved in a crouch now, gambling that this would be the last-ditch trap.

I was right.

When I got to the door I did a careful sweep but there were no trip wires and so I eased it open with my heart beating like a triphammer, praying on one hand I'd find Maria on the other side, and on the other hand terrified *how* I would find her!

Chapter Twenty
AN END TO PAIN

The door let us out behind the house to a dirt road across from the dark bulk of a pseudo-Tudor style boathouse. The moon was up and full so the whole scene was bathed in blue-white light that cast shadows deep enough for a dozen assassins to hide in.

The others came out of the door behind me and hugged the wall of the mansion, regarding, as I did, the bare space ahead of us before the boathouse as a kill zone. Anyone crossing it would be exposed to someone in the shadows of the other building with no cover at all. We would be sitting ducks.

"What do we do now?" Maxim asked in a shaken tone.

The traps inside had rattled him, and I don't blame him. I'd been through that sort of thing in Fallujah and the Anbar Province. Coming to fear every step shakes up your worldview at first. Sad to say, you get used to it. Probably the other definition of PTSD, that you come to expect it.

"Wait here," I answered as calmly as I could. "Let me make the run; if I make it okay then follow quickly." Before he could say anything I bent double and ran across the space in a zig-zag pattern as fast as I could.

I raced across the open space, my heart pounding, the image of Maria's terrified face floating before me. I tried to starve my mind to what that madman Carter might be doing with her, thinking only of holding her in my arms again. All my doubts were gone as I tried to imagine life from that point on without her and found I couldn't.

I knew that Maria was the missing piece of me, I knew that with certainty and was determined to not mess things up like I had in college. I was a different person now and I hoped that would make the difference.

Just as I got to the door I heard Maria scream, "No, William, no!" from the other side of it. "Don't do it," then there was a gunshot.

"Maria!" I yelled as I threw my shoulder against the stout oak door. Then a second gunshot sounded.

I jammed my shoulder into the door again and tried to wrench it open but it was barred solid.

"Maria," I yelled, "I'm here, hold on!"

The others had run across the open space now from the main building with Maxim yelling, "Did I hear Maria?"

I set myself to kick it open when there was a sudden whooshing sound and then the door blew off its hinges, ramming into me and sending me flying backward as a massive explosion ripped though the entire building.

The others were thrown to the ground hard enough to knock the wind out of them.

I was dazed. My ears—still ringing from the bomb in the main building—now went all but deaf. The door landed on me and I banged my head hard on the ground.

The night erupted into a volcano of flame that vomited out the open doorway and from the windows of the boathouse with flaming debris showering down on all of us.

It was like a slow-motion silent movie as the pieces of the building rained down all around me, the door taking hits from a twisted piece of end-wrought iron that would have killed me if it had hit me directly.

Maxim came crawling to me, putting a big ham hock of a hand on my shoulder and leaning in to yell.

I think Maxim said, "Boat fuel!" but couldn't tell for sure. It figured, however as there were multiple and continuous ignitions after the first explosion in a chain of ever-increasing fury.

I pushed the door off me and struggled to my feet. I was dizzy and stood swaying, staring at the Armageddon before me while flaming debris continued to rain down all around me.

"Maria!" I screamed without being able to hear my own pleading voice.

I headed for the open doorway but the belching flames drove me back. I frantically raced up and down the front of the building trying to find a way in.

After what seemed like an eternity I couldn't take it anymore and took a deep breath and headed straight for the blown doorway when it seemed the flames had subsided a bit.

I made it only a foot or two inside before a gust of flame slammed into me and I had to throw my arms in front of my face to keep from being blinded. I tried again, but someone dragged me away as my clothes and hair caught on fire.

Maxim and Harvey Walters slapped out the flames on me and the big Viking sat on me as I screamed "Maria!" over and over. There was nothing I could do.

There was nothing anyone could do.

The boathouse continued a series of explosions for hours. When the late-arriving fire departments from three towns around got to the scene it was all they could do to hose down the main house to keep it from igniting as well. It took a night and a day for the local departments to get the fire completely out as the stored fuel kept reigniting. By then all that was left of the building was a smoldering black smudge and a lot of memories.

I had second-degree burns on my hands and forearms, and minor burns on my back and legs. I lost my eyebrows and had some damage to my lungs from smoke inhalation. And I think I lost my mind as well.

They had to sedate me, they said for the pain in the burns, but I think I scared them with how I behaved after it was clear that Maria was dead. It is always a tricky thing for an ex-drunk, being given drugs as I have an addictive personality; there is always the danger that I'd end up with a bigger problem, but I was so far gone I really couldn't protest. I have only the haziest memories of screaming till my voice was hoarse.

•••

My mother came for me when I called her from a hospital three days later and said nothing. Nothing. I think her silence about the whole thing was the worst.

She took me home on a private plane supplied by an old friend of my father's and nursed me back to health herself with all the foul-tasting and smelling traditional remedies that worked three times faster than western medicine.

She never once mentioned Sammo or even Maria but the ghost of that dark-haired woman hovered between us my entire recovery period.

I didn't sleep well, at first because of the pain of the burns then, as the drugs that made the physical pain bearable allowed some rest, because of nightmares. I kept hearing Maria scream, kept hearing the gunshots and feeling the flames blast into me again.

Over and over.

Even I realized it was obsessive, but I could not stop the loop of sound and images from playing in my head again and again.

Once I was past the bed rest and drugged sleep stage my mother had me on the mend quickly whether I wanted it or not. On top of all her ointments and special soups she had me doing a reduced workout daily within two weeks. She knew better than to work me out herself (honestly she probably would have beaten me to death with her work ethic) so she called in Danni Shaw.

Danni was a tall, muscular Amazon who had saved my life overseas several times, as I suppose I had hers, since we were a tight knit in the squad. She'd come out to me on a rooftop in Fallujah and ultimately left the Corps to marry the love of her life, Emily. I'd wanted her to hold out leaving the Marines till things changed with 'don't ask, don't tell,' but ultimately I couldn't blame her for wanting to live openly as who she was.

We'd stayed in touch afterward and I'd been able to help out a bit after we were both separated from service. She worked in private security now and I'd even hired her a few times for jobs for the Shadows Foundation, as well as Emily, who was an accountant and a computer whiz in her own right.

She and her wife Emily came running when Mama-san called them to tell them what had happened to me. Once I was up and around Mom asked Danni to put me through my paces.

I think, actually Mom called Danni so she could play video games with Emily while her redheaded wife worked me until I was too exhausted to move at the end of each day.

If anyone had the right and the ability to stick it to me, it was Danni. Which she did. In spades.

"You have no blame, Jon," Danni said as she pushed me to do a third set of two hundred push-ups. I did them on my fists so they did double duty, toughening my knuckles and keeping pressure off my wrists. My hands were tender, but Mom's salve had allowed me to heal at a rapid rate. Danni worked on my mind while she worked on my body each day. "You did everything you could have to save her."

"No," I protested as I pushed hard, my muscles burning by number sixty this time. "Obviously; I could have kept her out of there. I could have put a bullet in that sick fuck's head the second he pulled those yakuza out of his butt. I could have—"

"Stop it now, Marine," Danni ordered with a gunney's authority. She stepped to a cabinet to pull out some focus mitts and motioned me to get up. "Give me a combination, leatherneck. Now."

I rose and carefully put on some fingerless Kempo gloves and started to hit the focus mitts as she held them up. She moved them side to side and up and down and I fell into a pattern—jab, jab, cross, uppercut, picking up speed then she shifted on me.

We worked hard for three three-minute rounds with her shifting pattern so I had to adapt. By the third round she was backpedaling and making me move as well. My arms felt like lead and I thought I'd pass out for want of air but I followed the advice of my old *Sulsa Do* teacher, 'when you are tired is when you have to work harder' and I put all I had into that punches.

She said, "Ding!" and my arms dropped. I swear I couldn't have lifted them again if Godzilla came at me at that point.

"I thought I stood a better chance of survival with you than Mama-san," I said, "but now…"

Danni smiled like a top sergeant. "Well, I have to make up for that forced march in Kandahar."

"That's dirty pool!" I was about to quip again, but Mama-san came sweeping in and stopped at the door to the *dojang*.

"Sweating, good!" she said. "Go wash and then to your father's office; I just got the police reports from the fire."

Chapter Twenty-One
A PUZZLE BOX IS A COFFIN

Fifteen minutes later, wearing a robe and with my hair still wet from the shower I was in my office. It had been my dad's but I'd been using it for eight years, though Mom still referred to it as Dad's. Emily and Danni were there with Mom sitting behind the big desk, looking even tinier that usual.

On the desk in front of her was the coroner's inquest report and a folder that had the FBI logo on it.

I had been to the coroner's inquest, even if I wasn't my old self and the inquest panel laid things out pretty clearly: a verdict of murder (Maria Carter) and suicide (William Jonas Carter) with a side of intentional arson.

Mom had used her contacts in the government to get more detailed information and, considering that William Carter was under investigation from the FCC, the Secret Service and the FBI there was a wealth of information to be had; more, in fact than I had originally gotten from the CIA.

My first supposition that the boat fuel had been what burned so hot and went up was true; there were no explosives as such, no Semtex or dynamite. The fuel had burned hot enough so that there was precious little of my Maria left except ash, some hair, two teeth and part of one finger—determined to be her left pinky. It was more than enough to identify her.

Stay professional I told myself as I looked through the paperwork. Danni and Emily both read the folder as well, but I was sure they were looking at my reaction as much as they were studying the paperwork. Mom had already memorized the whole jacket before I opened it to look.

With the way fire can be capricious, William was charred but not reduced to the pile of ashes that Maria was, with enough of his skull to see a nice clean bullet hole in his right temple and the melted frame of a pistol in what was left of his right hand. There was not much else left of him but it was enough to identify him by his bridgework, and ring. There was enough for a DNA match with samples from his brushes, toothbrush and the like in the house.

The surviving Japanese thug was covered in tattoos that indentified him as a yakuza stooge for hire out of Osaka but the Japanese police had no actual record of him. He refused to say anything about anything so was being held by Homeland Security till somebody could figure out exactly what to do with him. My suspicion was that he was subcontracted to the Kobe Yamaguchi-gumi in hopes of graining status and becoming a 'made man' as it were, in the yakuza world.

"Carter sure seems to have worked on his scheme for quite a while," Emily said. She was smaller than Danni, with mousy brown hair, a gentle demeanor and intelligent, shining eyes. "The SEC investigation shows that Carter had all but emptied the Phools' portfolio over a four-year period with switchback and cut offs. It is really brilliant. It definitely began before his car accident."

"If there really was an accident," I said. The others looked at me but I just shrugged. "You have to wonder, did it really happen or did he fake all of it to allow him to stay isolated and give him an excuse for…erratic behavior?"

"From what you said," Danni remarked, "he was pretty far gone in the realms of the insanity by the end—"

"Well, whatever he became, he was cunning about his finances," Emily said. "Maybe something finally snapped. Maybe it was seeing you with her, Jon, that set him off. Who knows?"

When they saw the look on my face, Danni added, "But there is no way to say that is what did it, Jon. You said, yourself, he had tried to kill her before she came to you."

"Yes, I know. But it is not having a real answer. There are police reports on the accident, but they could have been faked, or exaggerated—God knows he had the money to bribe local yokels to support any story he wanted to tell. It's just, well, not knowing for sure about if I was the trigger or not that is the hardest. Why? Why? It just keeps chewing at the edges of my consciousness."

"You think too much," Mama-san raised eyebrow. "Action is what you need to do."

I looked at her a little confused; she had not said much to me the last couple of weeks, beyond normal household conversation; absolutely nothing pertaining to Maria or the whole thing at Carter's. Now she was implying something.

"What action?" I kept going back to the reports and trying to find some clue as to Carter's real state of mind or when he had 'turned.'

Mom looked at me with what was supposed to be an inscrutable expression but I knew her too well; she had seen something in the reports I had not, something that got her devious mind working. That was always bad news for somebody.

I pulled up the FBI report and looked at it again but couldn't find that pebble in the shoe.

"What, *Haha*?"

"The condition of the two bodies," she said. "How could one be burned so badly leaving only ash and one not? They were found close by one another."

"Fire can do that," Danni offered. "I've seen it in Afghanistan. It can be very capricious with no apparent logic to it."

"Sometimes," my mother now very much the life long *kunoichi*. "But this is too convenient. It was as if fuel was poured on the girl and not him… except where it mattered."

I thought about it and suddenly saw where her devious mind was going.

"Of course, I see what you are implying. If I was going to fake my death I'd think about what was needed to identify me; fingerprints, teeth, DNA. But—"

"If the FBI are convinced that Carter is dead, why would you not be?" Danni asked.

"Because police organizations think inside little boxes," Mama-san said. "They like to end cases. Close files. But if this man took his own life after all this planning of death traps and gathering everyone together it seems foolish to think he would kill himself in so haphazard a way."

"And," I continued her train of thought, "Why have they not found the money?"

"I see," Emily said. "If he planned to die with his penchant for all the theatre he put on, why bother to hide the money he had stolen? Why take these precautions at all?"

"But how do you fake all those things?" Danni questioned. "They found his skeleton…badly burned, but it was there."

"Well, they had no fingerprints to go by on him," I pointed out. "He never served or was arrested. Maria had a security clearance for some coding work she did for the Air Force ten years ago which is why they know it. The DNA in the ashes matched; it was her finger."

"They were able to get his DNA from his toothbrush and a lock of hair in his personal bathroom that matched that of the charred body they found. And the teeth." Emily said.

"There were records of that for various legal matters of height and weight and all that," I added. "But the teeth, the DNA and the clothes are not all that is needed." I sat on the edge of the desk and picked up the photo of Carter as he was before his accident and stared at it.

"If you were rich enough you find a body double, then you fake an accident so you don't have to worry about how exactly that double matches. Maybe even get a guy with wounds that are similar to yours, and you have the guy's teeth altered to match yours so it's the same bridge. Then you have him use your toothbrush and comb for weeks before the event. He lives like a king while you live in the shadows and meanwhile shift all your money into phantom accounts."

They stared at me and Mom like we were insane but I continued, "You have that person use the toothbrush and comb that you know the FBI are going to get their DNA from. Then when you want to vanish you arrange for a high drama way for him to die and at the same time you take out your unfaithful wife." I was all professional now, not thinking of it being Maria, but seeing the scheme as something I would plan if I were trying to dodge capture; exactly as Mom had taught me all my life.

"So he takes her into the boathouse, knocks her out. The double was already there, probably with some of the yakuza; since no drugs were in his system I'm assuming they did sleeper hold on him so he was naturally unconscious; an expert could put him out safely and keep him out as long as you needed with no marks on him. You shoot the wife then pour fuel on her and light her while she is still alive, then you put a gun into the double's hand and make him shoot himself in the head. As a final touch you use a hand torch to burn off your double's fingers and char a good deal of him leaving all the 'good parts' for us to use to identify him. All this is done in minutes. Then you slip away and leave all the officials with egg on their faces and me with a weight of guilt that would make Atlas collapse."

We four sat there for a few moments while everything I'd laid out sunk in. Everyone was obviously mulling it over. Finally I summed up the obvious, "That bastard staged all of it; just like Agent Burton set the fire to cover Sammo's murder."

"How do you prove it?" Danni asked.

"Always trace the money trails," Emily said. "There has to be some record, somewhere out there where he put it; if he were going to come back from the dead he would have to have some identity or company he transferred it to."

"The SEC and the others are looking at that," Danni reminded us.

"But not from this angle," Emily said, "They are looking for where he put it assuming he was going to be carrying on before he went crazy…not for a man that was setting up a new life under a new name perhaps halfway across the world."

"Do you think you can find the money?" I asked Emily.

"Em' can find anything," Danni said with a smile. "She is with a keystroke what you are with an M16, Jon." This made the brunette woman blush but she smiled at her wife and nodded.

"Given enough time and a better computer set up that you have here, I think I can find it," she said.

"And I will have our relatives look into the Japanese connection to this," Mama-san said. She looked at me and nodded. "Vengeance is better than moping. Dae Hoon deserves that."

I had to agree with her; it seemed that William Carter was out there somewhere and he had killed the love of my life and had my cousin killed. I was going find the son-of-a-bitch, because I was angry now. Very angry. That seemed to please Mom and this time, I didn't argue.

When a Shadows gets angry, things get done and people die!

Chapter Twenty-Two
BLOODHOUND TRAIL

Emily, with information Mom's contacts got to her, began the long process of ferreting out the financial trail of the now-ghosting billionaire. Mama-san put out the word with family in Japan to try and trace the yakuza who had worked for Carter as a back trail to where he might have gone, the reasoning being he would still need goons in whatever new identity he assumed and if he had been laundering money for a yakuza gang or gangs he might maintain the contact.

I continued to heal in both mind and body though both took longer than I could have ever imagined. In a couple of months I got past needing Danni's workouts to motivate me now that I had a purpose beyond simply healing. Now I needed to be in shape for when I found William Carter and nail his ass to the wall.

As soon as I could I attended twelve-step meetings because in the moments between hard workouts and exhausted sleep the doubts came back; not fast enough, not stable enough, not smart enough to know that Carter was a two-faced killer. Not good enough to save Maria.

That echoed in my head like the tolls of a funeral bell.

And that knell rang day and night in a chorus of voices and faces; my guys I'd lost in combat, the men I had killed in country and since, Sammo and most of all Maria's images floated before me whenever I closed my eyes.

Lots of meetings; not just my twelve-step ones, but a vet's group I had gone to periodically since mustering out as well. Those guys and gals understood.

I even moved on to other short-term jobs as I pulled myself together but with my eye on a future confrontation. I did not let any of my official contacts know what my suspicions were because, frankly, I didn't want anyone getting to Carter before I did. I needed to be in on the kill.

During all this time my mother never actually talked about Maria, Carter or the case, specifically, though she kept an eye on my training progress, occasionally offering actual advice as opposed to disgusted critique, which was the usual form of advice around the house.

And I went over the paperwork as it came in almost daily, combing through the various agency reports looking for any clue that might lead me to Carter and waiting for the financial thread that Emily might find to lead me to my prey.

I did find one piece of corroborating evidence a few weeks into my search; two months before the fire William Carter purchased a second dental bridge, claiming he had damaged one but nowhere in the vast inventory of his holdings that was exhaustively compiled by the very detailed-oriented FBI was that second bridge to be found.

Then five months after Maria was murdered I got a phone call from Emily.

"Jon," she said, "I found it."

"Yes?"

"A shell company that traces down a line of shell companies but ends up at a French-Germany based company."

"You're sure?"

"As I can be."

"I'll meet you and Danni for lunch around one. I have some plans to make."

"You're not going to turn this information over to the government? You're going after him yourself, aren't you?"

I didn't answer for a moment then, "So, one o'clock good for lunch?"

•••

I had my back to a wall in a small alley off of Marseille's main thoroughfare, the wide boulevard called the *Canebiere* and I had some serious concerns about making it out of that alley alive.

The rain was pouring down like it would never stop in the Vieux Port quarter of the city near the *Réformés* quarter. It was ten days after my lunch with Danni and Emily and I had chafed at even waiting that long, but there were arrangements to make and feelers to put out.

So I had made those arrangements and felt all I could feel and now I was there to meet a contact of a contact who said he had some information on what hole William Carter had disappeared into.

Jean-Claude was the name the contact had given me who had promised some of the Carter's secrets. Emily, whose computer security skills really were extraordinary, had traced several cut-off corporations and shell companies to a car rental firm where a big chunk of Carter's money had gone, but old JC had not kept the appointment. In his place three rough-looking fellows had shown up and had me backed against the damp stone of the alley wall.

"Okay, guys," I said in French with as wide a smile as I could muster. "I

"How do you prove it?"

am not the person you want to mess with. I need the exercise too much." I was not really myself yet, at least I had not been able to do full on workouts and some of my healing skin on my burns still stung, but there is nothing like on the job testing to see if I was up to the job.

The thug nearest me, a broad-shouldered fellow that looked to have north African blood grunted and grinned, showcasing two gold teeth. His pig-like eyes set beneath thick brows were shining with the joy of my upcoming stomping. He was clearly the leader of the trio.

"The boss said you would be a talkative one," the leader said in gutter French. "And that we shouldn't listen to your talk."

"Well, the boss wouldn't happen to be a guy named Carter, would it?" I asked. I knew that the phantom billionaire wouldn't be using his old identity, had probably had plastic surgery, but sometimes you lob a grenade and hope. Horseshoes and hand grenades, you know?

The troglodyte leader had apparently exhausted either his vocabulary or his patience for he waved to the other two thugs and they moved at me.

Both men were of the same sort as their chief, one dark of skin, beard and hair and one a skin-headed Viking. It was the bearded giant who came at me first with a long bailing hook in his hand. His scarred face was lit in a primordial grin that mirrored his leader's joy in the impending violence.

I really was not in the mood for that. I had no gun with me, as the paperwork wasn't worth it for just an exploratory trip to France, but I've never really relied on guns anyway. If you rely on any weapon you are admitting weakness; weapons can fail. The truth of combat is to *be* the weapon and consider things like guns, knives and bombs to be add-ons.

And frankly I had not had any real action since the fire and there was a part of me that wanted to test myself; these poor fools were just in the wrong place at the right time for that.

The bearded behemoth lunged at me with a sweeping overhead strike with his hook. I stepped in toward him and blocked the forearm while I jabbed two stiffened fingers into his solar plexus.

The lout stopped abruptly and doubled over with a silent coughing fit.

His bald compatriot had an ugly-looking knife and he certainly knew how to use it. In fact he seemed very eager to use it. He sidestepped the bearded one as the first man doubled over and lunged to slash at my midsection.

I dodged the first slash and snapped my wrist to strike Baldy directly on the back of his hand at a nerve center. It was a sharp rap and it caused him to yelp in pain and drop the knife.

I followed up my attack with a Korean-style spinning heel kick that hit him like a scimitar and smashed my heel into his temple. He dropped as if poleaxed.

It was only their leader and me now and he was ready to do the dance.

"Now, you want to tell me who hired you, pretty boy? I promise you a little conversation will save you some lumps."

The gold-toothed troll was having none of my conversation. He produced an old-time boarding axe from somewhere on his person and brandished it. He lowered his head so that he gazed at me from beneath his beetled brows and gave a grunt of challenge. Then, raising the axe over his head like a mad timberjack, he charged.

As the thug sprang at me I threw my right shoulder forward, twisted my hips and snapped out a simple sidekick to full extension. My booted foot hit him dead center of his chest with a sound not unlike a gunshot. He didn't even have air for a curse before he went flying back to sprawl on the wet cobbles and was out of it.

All at once I was standing alone with only the sound of the bearded goon's wheezing to compete with the sounds of the steady drizzle and the distant warning bells from Fort Saint-Nicolas.

I shouldn't have, but I felt good. Good to knock the rust off in something beyond a hard workout with Danni or one of my regular sparring partners. No matter how you think they will not hold back or take into account you are healing from injuries you can never be sure. These jokers didn't know me from Adam and sure as hell gave it their best; it just wasn't good enough.

"Okay, buddy," I said as I stepped over the fallen leader to tap my first attacker on the shoulder. "Perhaps you will tell where the man who hired you might be found?"

The pig-eyed thug stared hate at me. He gasped hard enough that he couldn't summon enough air to curse me though it was clear he wanted to.

"Now, now," I said. "Cheer up, pal. I just want a few directions then I'll be on my way. If not I might just get a bit annoyed." I did my best to assume the fierce look my mom used on me. "You really would not like to annoy me, pal, I promise."

Out in the Bay of Marseille the four islands of the Frioul Archipelago were barely visible in the fog. I could see the Quai des Belges at the end of the harbor that was the site of the daily fish market. Its aroma added to the pungent smell of the wild city's waterfront. I'm sure some of that was coming directly from my prisoner. I kept up my Mama-san look and waited while the thug considered what annoying me would look like considering his two pals were out cold.

"A man named Froutte in Callenlongue," the goon stammered in a whisper. "It's a small fishing village to the east." He looked suddenly shy and even humble and added, "You can't tell them you got this from me. He will kill me; I swear it wer'n't nothin' personal."

"Don't worry, no one will know you told me," I rapped him on the skull and dropped him unconscious beside his buddies. "You really must think I'm as dumb as you, pal."

"You need to train harder," my mother said, tottering out of the shadows down the ally, a bow in one hand and three arrows in the other. "Your timing was terrible with those three fools. Stop wasting time, I want to get back for some pastry with Emily."

Mother love is wonderful, ain't it?

Chapter Twenty-Three
THREADS AND TRAILS

I pulled out the cell cloner that Emily had given me and went through each of the goon's pockets till I found their phones. Electronic interrogation was so much more fruitful these days than rubber hose questionings.

Mama-san and I headed back to the more 'civilized' areas of the city to the hotel where Danni and Emily were waiting with croissants and hot chocolate for us.

"False alarm?" Danni asked me when we entered the suite we were occupying. We each had our own bedrooms off the central room and the whole place reeked of old world charm and poor French plumbing.

"Not really. Somebody defiantly put them onto me for asking questions about Franco-World Enterprises; they did not want me following the trail."

"He was sloppy," Mom said as she wolfed down two croissants that she dipped into the chocolate drink. "You need to train him harder, Danni."

The statuesque redhead giggled like a little girl and sat back in one of the over-stuffed chairs, stretching her long legs before her. "I think you're exaggerating, Ondine."

Mom just 'harrumphed!' and kept stuffing her face.

Emily took the cloner from me. "Get them all?"

"Only two of them had cell phones."

"Well, we shall see what we see," she said. She eagerly plugged the cloner into the laptops she had set up on a table in the sitting room. I have some computer skills but she really was a tech-ninja and I was glad she and Danni were along. Not that I could have stopped them.

I had tried to talk Danni and Emily out of coming with me but I might as well have tried to stop Mom. "Like you say, 'in for a penny and for a pound,'" Danni said. I knew better than to argue with three strong-willed women, and frankly I was glad for the backup.

Despite what I said to Mom I did feel slow with the three goons, unsure as I had not been for a long time. There is always a difference between even hard training and real combat, an adrenaline thing and a spiritual one that were as different as could be.

Hard training, the way Mom and my father and even the Corps advocated, with real danger and real consequences helped prepare one, but it was never the same. It is why good soldiers sometime froze or conversely untested or untrained ones came through in a pinch. It was in the soul.

I had the skill and the experience, but only life and death combat could test me. I had made it through my first test, but the three goons were not really the caliber of the yakuza I had faced at Sammo's. Honestly, I had doubts and doubts can kill you.

"Eureka," Emily cried with a gleeful smile. "I think we have a winner."

The three of us crowded over her shoulder and looked at the phone call log from the two cells.

"Not a single call to or from this Callenlongue," she said.

"Not that I expected him to be truthful, not really." I said, "Callenlongue is a picturesque little village with a lovely tavern and not much else to recommend it according to Google Earth."

"But there is a pattern of calls yesterday to Stuttgart, Germany."

"Why would a lower-level street thug be calling another country?" Danni asked.

"Especially since the calls were only yesterday," my mother said. "Four of them. The same day we landed here and began asking questions about that company."

"Yes," I agreed. "But I have to assume they didn't know it was me or they would have sent in the A-Team. That is was just had a standard order to discourage any questions—"

"Don't flatter yourself," Mom chided. "You were like a bloated cow in that fight."

"Thanks, Mama-san," I made a face. "Always there to bolster my crumbling ego."

"False confidence gets you killed," she said with finality.

She was right, of course. Damn it.

"So what do we do now?" Danni asked in an attempt to stop my brow-beating.

"I have not been to Germany for many years," my mother said. "I like the beer."

"Well, there you go," I surrendered. "We see what holdings that company has in Stuttgart and away we go."

•••

So that our little circus would not ring any alarm bells Danni and Emily traveled by themselves, flying; my mother took the train and I rented a car and drove (under one of my cover identities).

Mom had wanted to drive with me but I would rather have had root canal work and it was not too hard to dissuade her when I pointed out we would stand out too much as Asians if we were together.

"You are a terrible driver anyway," she shrugged. "And I like trains." There were times when I reminded myself she was named by her German loving father for a German water demon—Ondine—and she was more irritated than usual because she had to leave her little sidekick, Banzai back home. She obviously missed having the little noisemaker around.

So we made plans to rendezvous and split up with a strange sense of impending fate. Not something any of us, even Mom, could have put into words, but we knew we were getting close to our quarry.

"Watch your back, Marine," Danni said to me as she went down to get into her cab for the airport. "I didn't put you back together to see you damage my work."

"Oorah," I smiled. "I wouldn't dare disappoint you, soldier." She kissed me on the cheek.

Emily smiled up at me and leaned in, lowering her voice. "And be kind to your mom, she's worried about you."

That caught me a bit off guard, but I smiled and let her give me a hug. Both women got hearty hugs from Mom and then climbed into their ride and took off for their flight. They would do our first on the ground recon and have rooms ready for us when we got there.

Mom and I watched them pull away and it suddenly felt uncomfortable. We stood there for a long moment and I think Mom felt it as well. Without looking up at me she said, "You have good friends, Jonathan. Strong warriors; you can not let them down."

Now what the hell does that mean?

I looked over at her trying to find words. "Excuse me?"

"You must hold your anger close, and use it. Your enemy is cunning; we must stay alert to have vengeance."

"I will not shame you, *Haha*. Or father."

She gave a little bow to me. "I know. Now come get my bags. I want to get some croissants to take on the train."

•••

I did the drive to southern Germany in a relaxing two days. And while being relaxed when you are hunting a killer is a little dangerous state of mind to get into, it gave me too much time to think.

I thought about my drive back in northern New York with Maria and that got me in a really crappy state of mind.

"Gotta get your head out of your butt, Cuz," Sammo had said to me as we drove across Nebraska four years before in pursuit of a serial killer from an Indian Reservation. I had guessed wrong on which back road he would take in fleeing and we'd lost a half-day in chasing him. I was blaming myself.

"I know, Sammo, but I guessed wrong."

"So you guessed wrong. It happens. The thing is to not stick your mind there...like putting your mind in your weapon. Stay loose."

"I know," I repeated, "Keep your mind free. Still..."

Sammo punched me in the shoulder. "I'll tell your mother," he threatened.

"Okay, Sammo," I said aloud to myself as I crossed the frontier into Germany, "I'll stay loose. Damn, I miss you, Cuz; I swear I'll send the bastard that killed you to hell or die trying."

Chapter Twenty-Four
WATCH ON THE RHINE

Stuttgart is a pretty city, all the more so because it was essentially German's answer to Detroit at one point; home of the first Volkswagen, in fact. There are lots of parks among the buildings, most of which were rebuilt in the grand old style after the bombings of World War Two.

I'd spent time there when I was attached to a joint intelligence unit while in the Corps and knew the city pretty well. It was on the Neckar River in a valley called the Stuttgart Cauldron for the weather pattern that gets pretty warm in the summer.

I had booked a room in a bed and breakfast about two blocks from the hotel where Danni, Emily and my mom (in separate rooms on another floor) were staying. I drove directly to my room, checked in, did a stretching routine and had a hot bath before I called Danni on my burner cell phone.

"You guys up for a little skull session?" I asked. "I just arrived."

"Sure, we were just going to go out to dinner with your mom. Local German food?"

"Works for me. *Brauerigaststatte Dinkelacker* is really good; over on *Tuebinger Strausse.*"

"That's not far. Okay, fifteen minutes?"

"Good." I hung up and realized I was hungry for some good food. I had eaten pretty much the European version of fast food on my drive. It might seem strange to be thinking about something so mundane as a good meal with friends considering why we were in the city, but if there is anything I had learned in my life it was hold onto the little joys whenever you could.

The traditional restaurant was one I remembered from my time in the city, not too far from where we four were located and I knew that the others would arrive there in staggered, apparently casual form, so I ambled over myself by a zig-zag route. No matter how 'normal' the meal might feel I never lost sight of being on a 'job.'

It was early fall but the weather was not brisk yet; a light jacket was all I needed but I added a Tyrolean hat to give me a jaunty look (and down play my white hair). I took my time to be sure no one was on my tail, letting my natural paranoia work for me.

Satisfied I was on my own I actually made the restaurant ahead of my mom, but after Danni and Emily were already seated at a table at the back. I took note of the fact that they had a good view of the front door and were close enough to the exit if they had to. *"Well done, Marine,"* I thought.

I came in just as Danni was attempting to order. I say attempting, because she was trying out her German on the Czechoslovakian girl who was working as the waitress and who was totally stumped.

"Can I help, ladies?" I asked in English as I stepped up. My two friends played it perfectly.

"Yes, please," Emily looked frustrated. "We don't speak German and her English—"

"No problem," I had them tell me what they wanted and translated the order to German.

"Please join us," Danni invited. I acted shy, let them ask me again then ordered myself and sat down.

When the waitress had gone we all three laughed.

"Couldn't have planned that better," I said.

"And a plus that her English is not so good," Emily pointed out.

"Mama-san?" I asked.

"Right here," her voice came from directly behind me.

Damn, I never hear her.

"Well, hold the chair for me," she said. I stood and did just that and she slid in next to me.

"How was the drive?" Emily asked.

"Good, pretty country and once I got to Germany it was a pleasure to be able to floor it."

"Why I didn't want Danni driving," Emily grinned. "She'd be airborne in half a mile."

The waitress brought our drinks, local beer for the ladies and a cold coke for me. She took Mom's order—my mother spoke perfect German—then went away again. We chatted nonsense until our food arrived then got down to business.

"Have you been able to zero in any further on where the cell call came from?" I asked Emily.

"She has taken over the hotel room with her laptops," Danni said.

"The hotel has good wifi," Emily munched on a breadstick. "But I didn't trust it to not be hacked, so connected my own hotspot to use. Anyway, I was able to narrow the signal down to a cell tower near the riverfront, but with no more calls from that number I can't get it any more specific."

"Have you had a chance to see if there are any properties owned by that company near there?" I was enjoying the *schupfnudel* with *saurkraut* but I had to admit my mother's was better. She loved to cook German food as well as Korean and Japanese. The only thing she never really mastered was Italian food.

"Nothing in that area I can find," Emily said. "I hacked the town zoning regulations and there is nothing industrial with any company name linked to Carter's shell companies I can find."

My mom had *schweinshaxe*, a braised pork leg with a crunchy brown crust and was pouring gravy on it. "If it is near the river," she said between bites, "then perhaps it is something on the river and not the land."

"I hadn't thought of that," Danni admitted, "but if it was a boat it could be long gone by now."

"Still worth taking a look," I said. "It's all we have."

"We can take a stroll down there tomorrow morning," Danni said. "Totally the tourist thing to do."

"Yes," Mom agreed. "Technology is good, but human eyes are always better."

"Nothing else we can do tonight, then," I finished my plate just as everyone else did. "So let's enjoy it." I called the waitress over and ordered *Apfelkuchen* for everyone.

"Almost as good as yours, Mama-san," I said as we all wolfed down the apple pie.

"You better say that," she cautioned, "or you will never get any again."

The others looked at me for some snappy response but I just ignored the threat as I knew Mom liked to bake whenever she was annoyed, which meant she baked a lot. She would never withhold pie from me or anyone who wanted any. Empty threats are rare from assassins, so I enjoyed it when she made them.

•••

The four of us wandered along the shore of the Neckar River. It flowed through the center of the city and out into a fertile valley with lovely feudal castles along the way.

The riverfront was picturesque but I was not looking for lovely, I was looking for some sign of William Carter or a company linked to him. There were pleasure boats of varying sizes from sight-seeing dinghies to barges and various midsized cargo ships.

"Seems kind of pointless, Jon," Danni grumbled as we leaned against a railing overlooking the water in late afternoon. Mom and Emily were feeding breadcrumbs to pigeons along the wharf and seemed to be not troubled by a thing in the world.

"I know, Danni. I guess I had too much hope pinned on this; I thought well, maybe…"

"Don't get all dark again, Jon."

"I won't. I know he's out there somewhere." I scanned the river with no real hope of seeing anything at this point, all but resigned to my search for the 'dead' billionaire coming to an end for now. Then I spotted something.

"Emily," I called to Danni's wife. "You have your tablet with you?"

She looked up from a pack of birds that were clustered around her feet and nodded.

"Look up the registry of that boat," I said pointing to an 80-foot motor yacht in the middle of the river that was anchored out of the main channel. Emily pulled out her tablet computer and doodled around on it for few moments.

"Bingo," she said. "Owned by the Franco-World Enterprises registered in Bonn."

"How did you know?" Danni asked me.

"Only an egotist and a drama queen like Carter, would have the hubris to name his boat after the two-faced God, *The Janus*!

Chapter Twenty-Five
CLUB HOUSE

Once we had something to focus on we got things moving.

My 'credit' with the agency was good enough, and I had enough contacts that a few calls to Langley and a long conversation with Joyce where I explained what I had been doing and why—and got yelled at for my trouble—got me the new station head's name. Maysonet. Josh Maysonet.

Stuttgart is where the US Constabulary had its headquarters at Patch Barracks during occupation when the 7Th Army was based there. It was where I served with a joint intelligence task force for about six months between my deployments to the Middle East. I got to know the CIA station officer there, a guy named Turner who worked out of the Barracks. The new guy had the same office.

"Hello, Mister Shadows," Maysonet said with an extended hand. He had a firm handshake and a generic smile. "My pleasure to meet you; I must say your fame precedes you."

The room was small and grey with generic furniture and a few file cabinets that looked like they had seen better days. The chair he offered me had a fabric rip repaired with duct tape.

"Cut your station budget, haven't they?" I asked.

He shrugged. "The cold war comes and goes but with the administration cozying up to Moscow we're not seen as having all that much value now. That will change. Always does; sneaky is forever."

"That is true." We sat for a moment with the sound of the base outside filtering in through the poorly-insulated walls.

"So Langley says I make myself available, full deal. What can I do for you?"

"Well," I pulled out a piece of paper. "I have a little laundry list for you here. I'll be happy with any of it, if not all."

He looked the list up and down, made a few 'hmmm' noises and then said, "I think I can get most of this, though might have to substitute some generics for some of the eh…brand name…high end stuff."

"I ask for the sky but am happy with a little patch of dirt," I quoted an old Korean proverb. "Anything will be appreciated."

"You know the Agency will ask for its pound of flesh at the other end of this," he said with unexpected honesty. "I was told there was a possible big fish you are tracking down…"

"Oh, they own me already," I admitted, "but this if for them if it pans out. They know the fish I am after, so all is good."

"Give me your number and I'll call you when I get all this rounded up."

"Thanks," I said shaking his hand again. "I'll keep you in the loop."

"Oh, I know you will," he said with a more characteristic tone. "We all know that Uncle Sam is always watching, right?"

•••

"This is a family matter," my mother said. "You have no business bringing anyone else into this."

We were in her room at the hotel, having left Danni and Emily after I filled them in on my meeting with the company man. "Mama-san, there is no way we could get all that stuff on our own here and we need it to surveil that boat."

"We don't need toys to watch people—"

"But we do to listen on phone calls, and we do to get past the security of one of the top computer geniuses on the planet who has millions of dollars."

"The old way—"

"Will not work on the high tech equipment that computer genius who has fooled every one of the US government letter agencies." I was working hard not to raise my voice, because that would only get Mom to stonewall me.

"Emily can handle it," she argued.

"She is the one who asked me to get most of this equipment."

"We could have gotten it."

"Maybe. Eventually." We stood staring at each other for a long heartbeat and I knew what it was all about, so I said, in a softer voice, "*Haha*, I will not let the government stop me from doing what must be done."

"Yourself?"

"He killed Dae Hoon. And Maria. Do you think I would let anyone else wring the life from him?"

"You swear it?"

"I swear it on the love we both had for dad and I have for you."

That stopped her. She nodded, her features relaxing. "Make sure he knows it is you and that he suffers. He must suffer."

"I can promise you that."

"Good. It is the family's honor. Now go, I need my sleep."

I went to the door but as I opened it she said, "Be careful; the time to be alert is when it seems like success is in sight."

"'Nite, Mama-san."

"Good night, ungrateful child!"

•••

Maysonet called me by lunch the next day to tell me that most of the stuff we had asked for was ready to deliver. By then we had rented a small apartment over a store two blocks from where the yacht *Janus* was moored, with a clear view of the river. I had him drop the stuff off there.

Emily was taking great delight in playing Jane Bond and set up her dream surveillance room in the second-floor apartment. She had all the monitors and computers she needed to tap into any calls made to or from the yacht. She had already established that it was owned by the Franco-World Enterprises and I had found out the boat was the traveling home of someone called Count Vertigan. My research showed he was an Andorran national but I could find nothing going back more than five years on him.

"It is really in Carter's DNA to make himself into a count," I said when I discovered that fact. "He had planned this even before his car 'accident.'"

"But an Andorran?" Emily questioned.

"Small enough country to buy residency and create a back history," I said. "I'm surprised he didn't buy diplomatic immunity with the deal."

"Would have made him too high profile," Danni said. "But yes, a count? This jerk was born in Kansas City; probably wanted to be royalty all his life; from what you said he lived like it."

When I got to the rental, which was over a closed-for-renovation sweet shop, I saw that Danni had already helped Emily set up and was looking over the 'equipment' that the CIA guy had sent for me and her.

"Got almost everything," she assembled a thermal sniper scope. She had a Ruger sniper rifle with bipod and ammunition for it as well. She had set out most of the armament that Maysonet had sent over, pistols, holsters, ceramic knives and a several bricks of C4 explosives.

"Like Christmas at Sing Sing," I set to checking the weapons. There were cleaning kits with them all and she and I set about disassembling, cleaning and reassembling everything. Like two good little Marines we even checked the ammo to make sure they were all full loaded.

"That CIA guy is my favorite Dutch Uncle," Emily called from the maze of computer screens she had set up around herself. "He even got the acoustic 'guns' you asked for, Jon."

"I mounted the funnel for it on the roof," Danni said. "She has the swivel controls over by her."

"I'm gonna call this place the Batcave," Emily announced with glee.

"Geeze, you guys did an amazing job here." I walked over to the window where they had already set up a telescope that was pointed in the direction of the river. I could see *The Janus* sitting off the main channel near the center of the river. As I watched, a motor launch came out to it and several people boarded the yacht.

"There are some things that your guy didn't include," Danni said. "Some of the, uh, specialized stuff."

"You mean the old stuff, eh?" I saw the look on her face and I laughed. She shrugged.

"I mean, really. All that stuff is so…so…low tech."

"Worked in Kandahar," I said. She arched an eyebrow.

"What are you two talking about?" Emily asked without looking up from the keyboard she was tapping away at.

"Jon would sometimes ghost off base without a gun."

"I was going for intel and prisoners. Guns are fine for distance but they are noisy."

"It was a war zone, Jon," Danni reminded me. "Even if you don't use it you take a gun."

I shook my head. "Human instinct is if you have it you will use it; sling and bow and knife were enough."

At that moment Mom gave the entrance knock and Danni let her in. She was carrying a hockey equipment bag that almost dwarfed her.

"I went to your cousin Kentaro's School," she set the bag down and unzipped it. When she saw my expression she added, "When Danni said that government man could not find the important things I remembered that Yukio, Kengi's wife's sister, had a child who had a school in a suburb of this city."

She pulled out a dark grey Ninjitsu stealth suit, a folding bow, arrows, a blowgun and several other traditional tools of Ninpo. She held up a *tanto* and handed it to me. "It should be a family blade that ends this."

My mother did not take the concept of vengeance lightly; in that, I took after her and then some.

Chapter Twenty-Six
BIG SISTER IS WATCHING YOU

We spent three days once we had our set up our 'headquarters' just watching the yacht to gather intelligence. We had to be careful, since Carter was a genius with electronics and I imagine paranoid, but fortunately we had a secret weapon; Emily. It seems her computer skills had been wasted on simple security checks and accounting encryptions up to this point. I suspect, afterward she was going to get into the spy game full time!

I used a wetsuit and a re-breather to get under *The Janus* and physically attach a listening device to the hull that picked up sound vibrations. To avoid any chance of our transmitted signal being intercepted I ran a cable from the device to the bottom of the river and along that to a transmitter twenty yards out from the boat. The device had a failsafe in that it would tear free if the boat took off, but would not register on any bug detection device by virtue of being old school; no electronic bug signal to detect!

The microphones from the device allowed Emily to filter out the sounds of the engines and ambient boat noise through one of her computers and we were able to get a decent fidelity transmission of conversations in most of the compartments of the vessel.

Once we had the physical tap we could combine them with the laser listening device that aimed a beam of light, picked up vibrations off of the glass of the potholes and converted them back to sound. It gave us pretty much full coverage of the whole boat. When you added in Emily's intercepts of cell phone signals (which even the encrypted ones she 'untangled') we were able to listen to everything that went onboard the *Janus*.

And a lot did.

There was a steady stream of people going to and fro from the boat and dialogue in German, French, Dutch, English and Romanish (the official

"You swear it?"

language of the trilingual canton of Graubünden in Switzerland). Emily spoke French; my mother spoke all the rest but Romanish, though she recognized it.

We soon had a fair idea of the extent of Count Vertigan's empire; major holdings in at least four countries but minor ones in half a dozen more. Most of the holdings went back at least three years but some twice that. It was clear that Carter had long planned to pull a Lazarus act after he stole his 'friends' fortunes. How long ahead he had planned to kill Maria was anyone's guess.

As for Vertigan, Emily was able to get clean recordings of his voice several times and did an overlay with them to a verified phone call Carter made several years before to a government contractor (pays to have contacts) who had to record all conversations. The voiceprint was an exact match.

"We have the bastard," Emily gave out a little cry of triumph! Danni laughed at the uncharacteristic outburst from her wife, but Mom just looked at me with a serious expression.

"There can be no waiting now," Mom said quietly in Japanese. "It is certain he is there."

It was true. Vertigan/Carter had not left the boat in all that time and the recording we had for him was not from a cell phone. My actual sound bug had been what picked up his talking. Talking, giving orders, laughing (that burned me) and living the good life.

"I know, *Haha*," I said in English. "I will do what must be done."

"What does that mean?" Danni asked.

If she didn't know for sure, she had at least suspected where this was all going. She was, after all a smart lady and a Marine, but she was going to make me say it out loud. "You told State we were gonna lock this in, then turn him over to them, didn't you?"

I looked over at Emily and Danni and took a deep breath. I had dreaded this point in things because it was moving toward the endgame and it was going to go very much into a black op state of things.

"Ladies, I can not tell you how much all you have done to this point means to me…to my mom…to Dae Hoon, my cousin. To all my family. I lied to the Agency, but you didn't know so you have no guilt in that; you can get out of this free and clear."

They looked at me like I'd grown a second head.

"From this point out I think maybe you two should take a nice trip to Paris on us so…"

"What the hell are you talking about, Jon?" Danni demanded. "I meant what is the plan and how do we cover it up to the Agency. We're in this till you frag the son-of-a-bitch."

My mother snickered at my gobsmacked expression and Emily laughed.

"You've been getting slow, Marine," Danni chuckled. "Have to work you out harder next time."

I couldn't stop myself from grabbing her up off the ground in a hug which (considering she was only a couple of inches short of me and all muscle) wasn't easy.

When I put her down she noticed I was striving to catch my breath at the same time Emily was trying to stop laughing. "You worked too hard at that. Definitely have to work you out harder."

"Family," Mom smiled. We all had the realization that what she said was true and let it sink in.

"Uh," Emily finally breake the spell, "How are we going to dodge the law when you whack this guy, Jon?"

"Whack?" I laughed. "You have to stop Em' from seeing Scorsese films, Danni."

"Well?" Danni repeated. "How?"

"Well, that is still a little vague; but now we have four heads to put together on this instead of two we should have a plan in no time at all!"

•••

Actually it took us two days to come up with a plan that had any real chance of success and then only when one of the intercepted phone calls indicated that *The Janus* was getting set to head up river to one of Vertigan's holdings—a castle.

"It's not a great plan," Danni said when I explained it to her, "but it is something."

"Improvise, adapt and overcome," I shrugged.

"It has too many variables to be sure," Mom pointed out, "but it could work and that is better than letting him escape."

"Jon," Emily said, "You'll be alone—"

"Not really," I tried to ease her fears. "You'll be listening, and Danni will be ready to back me up."

"And me?" Mom asked.

"You can bake one of your *Apfelkuchen* pies for when I get back, Mama-san."

She swatted at me with a snarl and I jumped back.

"You are such a disappointment, child."
At least some parts of my life really stayed consistent.

Chapter Twenty-Seven
MY MOTHER, THE DISTRACTION!

I went into the water a little just before dawn wearing the rebreather and my dark grey stealth suit. The first part of the plan was simply to get on board, which, even though they had a deck watch was not as hard as you might think.

Yes, they had electronic defenses, but Mom took care of that by being a clumsy 'old German' lady out for a late boat ride who 'accidently' flooded her engine so her tiny boat 'drifted' into *The Janus* to give it a gentle bump.

It was enough to draw the on-deck security team and set off any proximity alarms so they had to turn them off to reset them. That was my cue—I scrambled up the side while Mom cursed in German and was in turn warned off and cursed back at in German.

In the near dark of the false dawn, with the floppy hat Mom had on they couldn't see her ethnicity, only her clearly tiny size. And they could clearly hear her colorful, native-accented language. Bad language was okay on the job, apparently, according to her, because I heard some stuff even I had not imagined. I would have to 'talk' to her about that. At length!

The guards yelled at her, she yelled back while she repeatedly attempted to restart the engine. It gave me more than enough time to make it to the deck and into the shadows of the cabin and into a door.

After what seemed like an eternity she got her engine roaring and headed away into the river.

"Crazy old woman," one of the security people said in French to another.

"Be glad to be out of the city for a while, Emile," the second guard said as the two of them resumed patrolling the deck. "It seems insane to spend so much time down here; it's so hard to keep the place buttoned up."

He was so right. Anyone with any real security brain would have kept their client in a nice safe hotel instead of where a wet ninja could get close. I worked my way down into the interior of the ship with only the sound of working crew beginning to make ready for departure up river. The passengers, and that meant Carter/Vertigan, were not stirring yet.

I had a pretty good idea of the layout from our sound taps and looking at plans of the same class of yacht, but real world is not the same as maps so it took me a couple of minutes to orient myself.

I knew that Carter's cabin was aft on B-deck so I moved back and down the companionway as swiftly as stealth would allow.

I wasn't as good as I needed to be, however, and my luck ran out.

When I reached the bottom of the stairs a crewman coming out of his cabin for a morning coffee saw me and yelled before I jumped him and knocked him out to silence him, but the damage was already done.

Crewmen and security men suddenly were everywhere. Two men were right behind coffee-man and I was able to take them out with two quick blows, but then the security team was on me.

Three men in battle dress uniforms and sidearms swarmed down the companionway right after me; my mom's distraction had obviously only put the gang on high alert and they must have been doing a sweep of the ship.

I took the first man with a ridge hand across the temple and the second with a grapple and a hip throw but number three, a big blond guy who looked like he bench pressed bulls for a workout, was on me in seconds.

I was slammed to the deck under three hundred pounds of private security who started yelling in Russian. I was tired of that circumstance so I hit a nerve center on his left bicep to allow me to slip out from his grip and swung up on his back to get him in a sleeper hold.

That was when the second wave of guards came on us and they hit me with a taser. First time didn't work except to cause me to lose my hold on the Russian bull lifter but they doubled down then tripled down and there was an infinity of pain, after which everything went black!

•••

I woke up naked and tied to a chair in an empty room that I was sure was deep in the belly of the boat. I had kind of expected that so I wasn't really surprised. I was sore from the tasers but a quick assessment turned up no other injuries. My captors had almost been gentle with me, except for a sore butt that told me they had done a full cavity search, thankfully while I was still out cold.

Odd thing about westerners, particularly Americans; they are so freaked out by nudity that they automatically assume that if they strip you they put you off balance and oddly enough Europeans have adopted the 'custom.'

It's not an issue with me; I was raised without that kind of body shame so when I came awake my concern was not my junk being on view but rather assessing how well I was tied (pretty good with my hands behind me fastened to the wooden chair back) and the state of the room (pretty bare with only another chair near the metal door and nothing else).

I studied the room and it wasn't promising; metal walls with no porthole, one other chair and one hatch that looked solidly dogged.

"This is another fine mess you've gotten me into," I said aloud. I wasn't just expressing my lack of faith in my own planning, I was making sure that if the boat was still anchored in the river and my audio taps were still attached that Emily would know I was alive. Just to be sure, and because I was a cruel person, I began to sing some Queen songs at the top of my lungs.

I had made it through "Champions of Love" and was well into "Princes of the Universe" before the dogging on the hatch moved and the door swung inward.

"Have you come to bring me a record contract?" I said to the broad-shouldered bull lifter who entered. He was not amused. Behind him came a second security guard who had a drawn pistol.

The two men stood to either side of the door and let a third figure in. He was dressed in a silk smoking jacket (with an honest to God ascot!), taupe pants, gold slippers and had a cigarette in a long ivory holder. He didn't look like any photos I had seen of Carter; his cheekbones were wider, his chin more square and his nose different, certainly done to fool facial recognition software. To be sure he had grown a beard along his jawline and had a goatee that made him look all the more like a cartoon image of a count but I could still see the telltale marks of the plastic surgery near the hairline.

His eyes, however, were the same as I had seen behind the skull mask in The Lair.

I didn't have to have much imagination to figure out who he was, but there was no reason to let him know that.

It took everything I had not to scream 'You son of a bitch, murdering bastard I'm going to tear your heart out!' as I thought of Maria dying by his hand and Dae Hoon dead from his hired thugs.

I heard my mother's voice in my head saying, 'Stay Professional.'

And I knew that was what I had to do so I simply said, "Count Vertigan, I presume?"

He gave a little laugh, one that was very much like the one he'd given at his lair in upstate New York when he was still William Carter.

His expression when he recognized me was priceless. He had the 'I know you,' face but he tried to play it cool when he said in a voice that did not even try to disguise his Midwestern speech pattern. "Who are you and why have to come onto my yacht; to kill me?"

"My but you must have a guilty mind, Count. As for me, it would be nice to be recognized," I said with a sad tone. "I'd shake your hand but..."

"Who are you and why are you here?" Carter said again with anger and a little fear in his tone. That made me feel good.

He puffed on his ridiculous cigarette holder trying desperately to be William Powell playing a 1930s movie's idea of a count being cool. I could see the wheels turning in his head wondering if I was there by coincidence or if a phalanx of police agencies were right behind me.

"I was just in the neighborhood and I thought I'd pop by for a cup of sugar."

Carter stepped in with a smile on his face and slapped me hard across my left cheek.

"Why did you come here?" He said, "You did not just happen on me; why are you here?"

I tasted blood from the slap but, frankly, I had been hit harder by beginners in a martial arts class.

I had to keep from smiling, knowing I had gotten under his skin. He really didn't know why I was there, if I had tumbled to his ruse or if I was working on some other case and it was coincidence. I knew he would have to find out before he offed me.

"I was just out walking my German shepherd and decided to take a swim, so I guess you better turn me over to the police; breaking and entering and all that, though I really didn't break anything."

He slapped me again, this time with a backhand.

"We'll see what kind of a smart-ass you are when Ivan gets you talking." With that he pointed to the bull lifter and said, "I'll get the captain to move us up river now. Call me when he talks sense."

Chapter Twenty-Eight
ALL AT SEA, UP THE CREEK

Ivan, as one would suspect, was not a subtle type. He kept asking me why I was there and what I knew and the usual things that bad guys ask when they catch you snooping around their secret lairs and getaway yachts. And he did it while punching me or slapping me with all his might.

While it was going on I felt the vibrations of the engines start and knew we were moving up the river to Carter the Count's castle so there was no point in me chatting for any eavesdropper's benefit anymore. I pretty much clammed up, which seemed to really annoy Ivan.

Not to be cavalier, but I had had experts work me over before and knew I could take a fair amount of that sort of unsubtle technique before I had to fold.

That being said, I'm pretty sure one punch cracked a rib. For the most part he was pretty good as that sort of interrogators go, causing pain on the muscular level but mostly nothing too serious. So cracking my rib was probably a slight mistake, not enough to take a gold star off his Torquemada rating for, in any case.

I knew it was just the beginning though; his kind would move to breaking fingers and toes in the not too distant future when he got frustrated with my silence.

Even if The Marine Corps had not put me through escape and evasion training and all that entails I still would have been ready for this kind of treatment because of my Uncle Kengi's training. There is a certain amount of physical pain that a human can take before the mind shuts down, or the nerve endings no longer send out reliable signals.

A good torturer (if there is such a thing) knows when to back off and let the victim heal, or at least recover enough to feel pain at full throttle again.

The CIA used to run a school for that sort of horror for Middle Eastern and South American allies—the US has the stain of a lot of vileness on its hands for El Salvador and Iran under the Shah—but they were amateurs compared to my Korean ancestors. The Korean conflict proved that; they had a much more 'get into your head' style of interrogation.

By the same token I had learned, via my father's *Sulsa Do* and my mother's *Ninpo*, a number of techniques to isolate my mind from the pain of most interrogations, a sort of autohypnosis. I didn't need it yet, as just the physical beating was still at the nascent stage and I really had taken harder hits in some of the more serious training sessions with Sammo or one or the other of my relatives.

I had stopped giving him clever retorts to his questions when the boat started moving. He was too thick-headed to get most of my jokes anyway.

That really did piss him off and he ratcheted up the abuse; but he was a professional so he still kept from doing any permanent damage (with the exception of that damn rib).

I was inwardly grinning, because it was clear that my presence had spooked Carter; he really didn't know if I had tricked on to him or was just involved in some investigation of 'Count Vertigan,' so I knew he could not really kill me for quite a while.

At least, I hoped Carter's crazy behavior at The Lair had been an act and he was smart enough to keep me around until he had definitive answer to what I knew and who knew what I knew.

Ivan took a break again after his fourth round of whack-a-Shadows, sitting in the other chair and knocking back a cold beer he had brought in with him. His blue eyes were shards of ice as he stared at me in a lame attempt to intimidate me. I suppose he wanted me to think about the horrible things he was contemplating doing to me but my mind went elsewhere.

"So, Ivan," I said. "*Spetsnaz?*" What can I say, I am curious.

He just stared at me over the rim of the bottle and I could see the tiny wheels under his beetle brows. Finally he just said, "*Da!*"

Made sense he was ex-Russian Special Forces, and I was pretty sure the others in Carter's employ would be ex-military as well; many thought merc work was honest!

There is a particular set of skills we have when we muster out and many turn Private Military Contractors to use them. To most it is just a job, at least above working as a mall cop. To me it was a family legacy that, admittedly I had originally tried to avoid.

To guys like Ivan it was clearly an addiction. He was a bully who liked the power a gun or a set of brass knuckles gave him; exactly the kind of man a loon like Carter would keep around him. He relished the chance to do the work he was doing on me and I knew in his ice-cold heart he hoped I would never crack and thus give him the opportunity to mess me up beyond repair.

"I worked with some of your guys when I trained in Systema a couple of years ago while I was still in the Corps," I said to keep things chummy. "They are pretty good with dancing; better than you are with this nonsense."

He started to get up with his Neanderthal face moving into a grimace.

"I just thought I'd save us both some trouble; I'm not gonna talk to you. I want to speak to Vertigan again. I'll tell him what he wants to know."

He looked at me like he was trying to decide if I was just stalling for time (which I was) or had something real to say to his boss. Finally he put the beer down and went out of the room, dogging the hatch behind him.

That left me with a little time on my hands to contemplate my circumstance. The boat was moving so my 'team' was going to have to be on the move as well, as we had planned. That meant that Emily would have a limited number of ways to keep track of me.

Mom would be furious I hadn't gotten off the boat with Carter's head in a bag at the first shot, but had thought that possibility was slim to none and besides, I knew I'd be able to rib her about her language as my diversion. Still, I was thinking hard exactly what to tell the rebuilt slime-ball when he showed up.

I had to keep him guessing while at the same time keep Ivan from improving his technique on me.

After about ten minutes I was bored enough to start singing again, which was interrupted in the middle of the second chorus of "Blue Suede Shoes" by the door opening.

"What do you have to tell me?" Count Carter shot at me the second he ducked into the room. "It had better be good."

"Good is a relative term, pal," I said. "I will tell you my name but you have to contact the U.S. Embassy. I demand you turn me over to the cops; I'll take my heat for the burglary rap."

I saw the veins on his forehead throb as he tried to control himself. "What the hell kind of crap is this?" He stepped closer and looked ready to slug me again.

"Sebastian Tombs, private investigator out of Philadelphia," I said. "And I was hired to investigate the Franco-World holdings in Belgium. I swear."

"Then why are you here?" He was doing a great job of pretending to not know me. It was a fun game, with me knowing who he was and him knowing who I was and both of us trying not to let the other know they knew.

I actually had to keep from laughing at his attempt to be a tough guy about it all.

"The trail led me here and I just follow leads."

"I will check that, Mister…eh…Tombs," he said. "Now tell me who hired you and why."

"I can't do that, man," I said acting insulted. "I have professional ethics; my clients paid for anonymity."

That did it; Count Carter was not going to put up with that.

"You're not funny, Mister Shadows. I know a lot more then you think."

Not so, ahole, I thought. *You just lost the 'I know what you don't know' game!*

He turned to Ivan. "Bag him and bring him up top. We will be docking in a few minutes."

With that Carter turned and left. Ivan grabbed a black bag and put it over my head, tying it tight at my neck.

Things were about to get serious.

Chapter Twenty-Nine
IN THE DUNGEON DEEP

They carried me, still tied to the wooden chair, up on deck of *The Janus*. The late morning air was cold and I could tell from the sound that we had reached Carter's castle several miles up river from Stuttgart. It was called 'Liebfreid's Lair' in the local dialect and it seemed appropriate for an egotist like the tech billionaire.

The goons carrying me like so much baggage were not gentle with my transport and I was lugged across a gangplank to solid ground and into what sounded to be an enclosed courtyard. After a couple of minutes I was indoors again and taken down some stairs into a small room. There they dumped me into a cold, dank room and left me with the bag over my head.

It was all intended to disorient and humiliate me, but I couldn't care less. I had guessed where he would take me and already knew the layout of the castle. My guess was that they dumped me in one of the lovely dungeons in the old place.

There they left me, with a loud slamming of a door and the very deliberate dropping of a bar across the outside of the door. Very theatrical.

All I could do was wait. All intended to discomfort me and soften me up for interrogation.

I almost laughed.

It was all standard technique so I just let myself go along for the ride. As a final gesture they poured a bucket of cold, brackish water on me that got me shivering so hard my teeth sounded like castanets.

I did my best to ignore the discomfort of my body and let my mind go inward to conserve my resources for when I needed them.

That let my mind wander…

"You ever think about how we were, Jon," Maria said as she lay on my chest after lovemaking. "I mean when we worked."

"That was a long time ago," I whispered. It was as if I didn't want to break the spell. It was our second night in the motel on the run after Sammo had been murdered.

"I know," she said. The scent of her perfume combined with the smell of our sex was a heady mix. "But I wanted to say that…that I have tried to see how much I hurt you and—"

"No," I said, "don't go there. We were both different people then. I wasn't who I should have been—"

"Now *you* stop that. I wasn't all that and a bag of chips, either." She giggled. "At least not spicy chips." She snuggled into me and kissed my chest.

I shivered; but wasn't sure if it was from the bucket of water now or from her touch then.

"No," I said in that hotel room. "I hadn't accepted who I was then; I wanted to be anything but what my father and mother had wanted. I was so selfish, it's no wonder you didn't want to be with me—"

"Stop that. I was pretty selfish as well. I only saw what was right there on the surface, Jon…not what was beyond. What could be."

"You saw it in William," I said and immediately regretted it. "I mean—"

"No," she said sharply. "He came along afterward, and you see how well that worked out. No hon, I saw only what and who you were then."

"Which wasn't much."

"No," she gave me a little punch to my arm. "You were in pain and I failed to see it. All the rebellion and self-destructive behavior."

"Well," I said with a wry smile, "that is a pretty accurate assessment of me at the time. "

"But I should have seen more, Jon. I should have seen more; who you could become."

"I didn't even know who I could become, Maria. I didn't find who I was until Kandahar. Until I saw what my father had talked about when I was training with those leathernecks, till I was crouched behind walls with people I suddenly knew would give their lives to protect me or any of those civilians and I realized I would do the same because someone had to. And I could."

"I should have seen that in you, Jon."

"How could you? It may not really have been there; I don't know." I pulled her close to me. "But it is ancient history. We have here, now. If I've learned anything it is to cherish what is, not what might be or has been."

"Cherish. I like that." She reached up to kiss me and I closed my eyes.

Suddenly the bag was yanked from my head and I found myself in a damp stone dungeon facing the new incarnation of William Carter as Count Vertigan.

Now he was dressed in a blue velvet jacket, gold vest, yellow shirt and red pants; he looked like a bad high school production of Barnum.

"Are you going insult me with your bullshit again, Shadows?" Carter said.

"Shadows?"

"Ivan!" he screamed and the blond monster stepped past him to slap me across the face hard enough that I saw stars.

"Don't give me any more crap, half-breed," Carter snarled. "I know who you are. Why are you investigating me?"

He still wasn't sure I was on to him and it was making him crazy to not know. Well, more crazy.

"That is for me to know," I hissed. "And you to—"

Bam! Another slap.

"Tell me!" Cater screamed. "What do you know?"

I smiled at him that I could see infuriated him, but he stopped Ivan from another attack to repeat, "Tell me or I swear you will not make it out of here alive. The men who built this castle built a way to get rid of trouble-some pests." He pointed to a grated and locked opening in the stone floor of the granite cell he held me in. "It empties directly into the river. With weights on your legs..."

My eyes went to the small, barred window high up on the wall that told me I was just below ground level. An actual dungeon; I felt honored.

"What exactly do you want to know?" I smiled.

I thought his head would explode when I spoke so casually.

"How the fuck do you come to be investigating me, Shadows?"

I played shocked that he knew my name. It was a game, but getting harder to play it with a chance to win.

"My name is—"

"Shut up!" he snapped. "I know you are that son-of-a-bitch half-breed Jon Shadows so stop trying to be smart. Why are you here?"

He fixed his eyes on me and I could see a bit of that madness that had been behind the skull mask at his old lair. I had to play it easy now.

"Do you think that you could appear with so many tendrils of crime and not be noticed, Vertigan?" I said. "Several people noticed and I got called in. Now I demand you contact the American Embassy to—"

"Shut up!" he screamed and slapped me again. "You will tell me the truth or you will end up dead."

I knew he was bullshitting me. He was gonna kill me regardless of what I said, it was just a matter of when.

"I demand to see a U.S. official."

"Ivan," Carter hissed. "Make him talk."

The blond goon grunted with joy and removed his shirt to reveal an upper body covered with tattoos. He flexed once to put on a show and stepped past his boss ready to lay into me.

Ivan froze when there was a sudden burst of machine gunfire followed by an explosion from somewhere outside the stone-walled room.

Chapter Thirty
STORMING THE CASTLE

Carter and Ivan both froze at the sound and I saw a panicked look flash across the resurrected tech-genius' face.

Carter turned to another uniformed guard who was standing near the thick oak door of the room and barked, "Find out what that is!"

"*Oui, Monsieur le Comte,*" the guard nodded and I could see he almost wanted to make a salute—he had not been out of the service very long at all.

The guard raced away.

Ivan, not one to let himself overthink anything, continued toward me and with no preamble laid into me again with open hands and fists, this time working a 'little deeper' than he had before.

My cracked ribs exploded with pain and he wasn't careful with below the belt blows either. I made up my mind that he would pay for his dedication to his craft—like I said, Mom wasn't the only one who believed in healthy retribution.

I saw stars and hissed in agony while Carter stood back and giggled.

I tasted blood from the beating and my left eye was swelling shut but nothing was damaged beyond a bad workout with Uncle Kengi, so I just smiled at my interrogator. That did not seem to please him.

"That all you got, Bonzo?" I asked in a hoarse whisper.

This set Ivan off again and he was starting another round when the French guard came running back with two others.

"*Monsieur Le' Comte,*" the guard stammered. "The castle is under attack!"

"What?"

"Two guards have been shot by a sniper, someone set fire to the fuel tanks on the north side of the building and the power—" Just then the room went dark as the overhead electric light, a naked bulb, went out.

"Find out what is going on!" Carter screamed. The light flickered back on as the backup generators kicked in.

"We have to get you to the safe room, *monsieur,*" the French guard urged him. "Now!"

"Yes, yes," Carter finally agreed. He looked daggers over at me then ordered Ivan, "Keep working; I want to know everything he knows now. No limits."

With that the resurrected 'Count' turned and headed out the door, pulling it closed behind him. I heard the bar drop and it was just me and my blond keeper.

"Do not talk, *tovarish*, I beg you," Ivan gleefully smiled. "Not for a very long time; I have faith you are a strong man. Do not disappoint me." He cracked his knuckles in his version of an intimidating gesture and stepped in to begin his fun.

Outside I could hear a mounting level of chaos, with screams and orders in German and French coming through the barred window at an escalating volume. All hell was breaking loose out there.

Ivan ignored the commotion and was really getting into the anticipation of ruining me, so he slowly walked to me in what I assume he thought was an ominous and menacing gait.

I judged that I had given the gang enough time to get things popping (I knew it was Danni that shot the guards) so I was ready for the next part of my plan.

When Ivan hauled back to hit me with a right cross he stepped in to do it which put his right shin in range of my left foot. Since my legs were not tied I had all the range I needed.

No matter how muscular a person is there are some places where there is very little muscle over the bone. One of them was the shin.

I snapped out what was a bastard low swing kick, twisting slightly to give it 'juice' and the ball of my foot smashed into his shinbone, which would have cracked his shin if I had a little more swing space.

I immediately snapped the outer ridge of my left foot in a semi-circle to slam into the bare bone.

Needless to say that hurt him like hell. He yelled and fell forward right at me. I twisted my body the other way and managed to hit him on the point of the jaw with my right kneecap. That blow torqued his head hard and he was out cold before he hit the ground.

"Wow, glass jaw," I said aloud. "Didn't see that coming, I was hoping to have to pummel you."

I rocked forward so my feet were on the floor with the chair on my back like a haversack. I waddled over to the unconscious goon and used my toes to go through his pockets. Nothing of use, not even a folding knife.

"You are useless, dude," I mean, what kind of amateur kidnapper uses hemp rope anymore to tie up a prisoner, anyway? Of course, if they had used zip-ties I could have snapped them (most people think you can't, but you can) but pros would have used handcuffs.

Outside I could hear several more explosions and continued small arms

Suddenly the bag was yanked from my head...

fire. I began to think I'd be late to the party if I didn't hurry.

I turned around from him and tipped myself on the chair's rear legs rocking back and forth to work the joints of the chair loose then when I was reasonably sure they were worked enough I let myself fall backward so that I dropped backward hard on his back, right over his kidneys.

This had three effects; one it made sure he stayed out quite a bit longer (and would probably piss blood when he woke up), the chair splintered so my hands came free and lastly my cracked rib hurt like a son-of-a-gun and I all but passed out from the pain.

After I got my wits about me and the red spots faded away I moved on to the other situation I was faced with, the locked door. Not a big problem.

As it was, I was free but any lock pick would not be of any use on the old mortis lock on the dungeon door or get rid of the bar on the outside.

Fortunately the solution was much simpler; I just knocked on the door.

"I'm done for now," I said in hoarse German to approximate Ivan's voice. After a moment the guard lifted the bar to let my interrogator out. As the door swung open I took the guard with a straight punch to his throat so he could not call out.

I grabbed him and pulled him into the room and choked him out.

It was my luck that he was about my size so I stripped him of his BDUs, and donned them. The shoes were nowhere near my size, being too big; that was okay, I was used to being barefoot. I filched his black watchcap and tucked my hair underneath it to complete as good a disguise as I was gonna get.

He also had a pistol and a Czech Scorpion sub-machinegun and ammo that would make things a bit smoother when I got into the party outside.

The guard had no radio though, which I found odd, but then, perhaps Carter prohibited them on site or had a radio blocker, as he had none on his yacht as well.

While I dressed the sounds of shouts and shots from outside increased even more.

"Nice job, Danni," I commented to no one just as a louder explosion than the others split the afternoon. That would be the yacht; the chunk of C4 explosive that Maysonet put in our Christmas package sure came in handy as a party favor.

"I guess its time for me to join the gala!"

Chapter Thirty-One
RAGNOROK

Leibfried's Lair was not a castle in the true classic sense. It had started as a conical watchtower of stone to keep an eye on shipping on the river in the 13th Century and had a stone building added some time later adjacent to it and then, still later, an enclosed courtyard.

Count Vertigan/Carter had added a garage and a generator shack with some fuel tanks beside it.

If things were going according to plan the first explosion had been the fuel tanks and the generator going; Danni had rifle grenades and incendiary bullets for those jobs.

The charge on the yacht I had set before boarding with Emily having the trigger to set it off when the moment seemed right. Bet she enjoyed that too.

Outside the stone cell was a dimly-lit corridor that had several other doors and stairs at the far end that looked to be going up to ground level. I was alone for about five steps then a uniformed guard came out of one of the doors. He all but ignored me (my 'disguise' worked) and headed up the stairs so I just followed at a run.

Turns out I had been held in the cellar of the stone house that abutted the tower. The guard ahead of me raced off toward the now burning garage while I veered around the building to head to the tower itself. Carter was sure to have his private quarters in the tower to satisfy his ego and it was a sure bet that would be where his safe room would be.

I was able to make it to the door of the tower unmolested but there were two guards posted there. I moved boldly toward them, calling out, "I have a message for the Count from Ivan," in French.

The guards hesitated for a moment and seemed about to answer when they noticed I wasn't wearing boots. So much for my disguise.

The one on the right went for his sidearm so I shot him in the head.

The second guard got his pistol out of the holster but I closed on him and used my own submachine gun to knock him to the ground.

"Tell me where the Count's safe room is," I snarled in French, "And you live to work for another employer."

The guy was in his late twenties and I would guess a Middle Eastern vet from the look of him. Maybe Foreign Legion. I could see he was ready to resist me 'for honor' and all that, but considering he was working for a skank like Carter I wasn't about to let him.

"This is not the Legion; you only owe him what you have given so far. Clam up and I will shoot your balls off but let you live to regret this. No one will know and it may not make a difference anyway. So tell me what I want to know and I will just knock you out. This is a soldier to soldier offer, limited time value though; I am in a rush." There was no equivocation in my tone and he knew it.

There are old warriors and bold warriors, but no old bold warriors. The guard decided to be an old one.

"His safe room is on the third floor," his eyes were focused on the muzzle of my Scorpion. "I don't know how to get in."

"No reason you should. Thanks. Next time check your employer out better and make sure he never pissed off a member of the Shadows family." I clocked him then and he went out cold.

The door behind the two guards was locked so I sat down on the back of the wise guard and reached down to the callous on my right heel. After a bit of work I began to peel it back.

One of the things about Ninjutsu is that it is as much a psychological art as a physical one. We do our best to understand the mind of people, to anticipate weaknesses and be realistic about it—why my mom, more than most moms, always seemed to be a mind reader.

So I knew that when people search you they do the usual—pat down, cavity search (which is not fun, unconscious or not) and run a metal detector over you in case you have some sort of implant. But feet—well, most people have a thing about feet so they only look in a cursory way.

And martial artist's feet are usually a very un-pretty mass of calluses. Mine were, but the heel calluses on both feet were actually fake—I shaved my real ones down and put an artificial skin over them with strong surgical glue. They looked and felt like the real stuff if you didn't explore too closely, which most people really avoid at all costs.

Under the 'skin' I had several carbon fiber lock picks, a small plastic blade and a filament line with finger loops that had been rubbed in diamond dust. If my hands had still been tied any other way than behind me in the chair I would have been able to use the blade in the heel to cut my bonds.

The door was not a problem; it was a moderately complex, modern lock, but still only took me a couple of minutes.

The Janus was going up in a series of explosions at this point, the C4 having set off the fuel in the boat and pieces of it were raining down all around the courtyard and pinging off the tower itself. Some of them were refrigerator-sized so I had to assume there had been other explosives on the boat as well.

Shrapnel started to ping into the ground and building all around me just as I got the door open. I dragged the French guard inside just as some metal pieces of the boat hull hit the ground near us.

"Hope you smarten up, buddy," I headed into the tower.

The interior of the stone building was dark, with the windows along the wall narrow and with thick, old leaded glass in them. They looked to have been arrow or rifle slits as one point that had been refitted.

As with most old towers the narrow curving stairs went up clockwise to impede attacking knights of old from swinging their right-handed swords and making it easier for the defenders to fight them. There were no such problems with submachine guns, so when two guards popped out and started to fire down on me I let them have it.

The second floor was a large living room office but was empty. I went up the flight to the third and kicked in the door to what was obviously Carter's bedroom-office that took up the whole floor.

It was made up like some old world bedroom with a huge canopy bed, a huge armoire, an antique desk and large, overstuffed chair. The one change he had made to the original structure was large picture windows he had set into the walls. One looked out over the river and I could see the flames and smoke from dissolving *Janus* with bits of it hitting the outer pane, which was clearly blast proof.

The other window faced the courtyard. The thick glass muffled the sounds but the explosions were continuing and I could see some of the hired help racing across the open space trying to get away from the yacht debris that was coming down on them. Some were stumbling and falling and though I could not hear it I knew it was from Danni's accurate fire from some treetop out in the woods.

As I watched, the outer wall of the courtyard suddenly exploded in a cloud of plaster and stone dust as a front loader barreled in through the wall. The giant road machine was cranking at full speed. I could not see into the cab because several bulletproof vests had been duct taped around the windows.

There were machine guns firing from the top of the cab and the front loader managed to rake the entire yard, driving madly around and chasing the screaming mercenaries like it was video game.

"Oh no, Mom!" It had to be her. She just couldn't sit back and let things take their own course.

"Better get this done quick," I told myself. I turned my attention to where the safe room had to be located.

The armoire would be the logical choice, but it was the obvious one so I went to the bed. The headboard was directly up against the wall.

"Eureka!" I cried aloud. "Come on out now, you weasel, or I will put a stick of C4 against the wall and blow you out."

As I set the Scorpion down on the bed to examine the headboard for the opening mechanism Ivan jumped me.

Chapter Thirty-Two
SHOWDOWN

The big Russian slammed into me like a bulldozer smashing me into the upright poster of the bed. My ribs exploded into agony.

Ivan got his arms around me from behind and squeezed me hard, yanking me off the bed and off the ground. I blew out all the air in my lungs and started to black out from the combination of the pain and lack of air.

"I will crush you, little man."

Not much for quips at that point, I bent my right knee and snapped my foot up hard into his future generations.

Ivan grunted, and though he did not release me his grip loosened enough for me to get free. I was able to squirm to the right so he was off my right shoulder. I slammed my head into his nose three times hard.

There was a spray of blood and Russian curses and his arms lost power so I pushed off him with my right arm, causing me to bounce on the bed.

He was right on me again but I kicked out to get a heel into his sternum hard enough to hear a crack.

More curses and he came back at me with a right cross. I blocked it with my left and hit him in the sternum again with a straight right.

That backed him up two steps and gave me enough space to shoot a low kick into the right shin again. He howled with pain as this time I had enough power in it to snap the bone cleanly.

The break had to be agonizing but the tough goon came at me pushing off his left leg and got his hands on my throat in a desperate Hail Mary attack. His fingers were like steel springs digging into my neck.

I knew it would be seconds before I blacked out so I pulled the pistol on my hip and shoved it into his chest to pull the trigger three times, blowing him off me. His last expression was a stunned questioning glance as if to say '*That's not fair!*'

"I'm a freaking ninja, bitch!" I yelled, "I don't have to play fair."

"Neither do I," Carter said as he fired a pistol from behind me, hitting me in the right forearm and right side. The bullets spun me around and disarmed me so that I hit the stone floor in a spray of blood and a sunburst of pain.

The faux count was standing at the open door to his safe room, a .38 pistol in his hand. His eyes were wide with anger and his mouth a twisted line. There was every bit of the madness in his expression that he had feigned in upstate New York.

"Now tell me why you came here, who sent you?" He screamed at me, his hand waving the gun like it was a pointer.

"Stop the act. I came here to get you, Carter, nobody sent me."

He almost staggered with the impact of my words. "How could you—"

"Come on, William. You may be a world class con man, but you didn't quite plan your death well enough. I followed the breadcrumbs."

"Who knows, who knows?" He stepped up closer so that the pistol was almost in my face.

I laughed at his growing terror. "Too many to let you sleep peacefully, Billy boy."

He snarled, "You're lying, you're lying!"

"What was it, William? Were your buddies in the Yamaguchi-gumi getting wise to you skimming money from them as well as from your Phirewall Phools?"

"Shut up!"

"Oh, you really shouldn't cross the Japanese mob, William. They have long memories. I mean, I'm a 'half-breed,' right, so I should know."

"Shut up!" He stepped in to put the gun directly against my forehead. A rookie mistake.

There are a number of disarms that depend on speed but all of them are based on the fact that reaction comes after action. In this case it would be his finger reacting to me moving.

The gun directly against a body made it easier since the bullet flies in a straight line so the person would only have to move a fraction to let the bullet pass him. Against a head, however, the percentages go way down. You have to be beyond desperate to try to do a disarm with a gun at your head; or angry. I was angry, but not stupid; something would have to happen for me to risk a disarm.

All I could do was keep working on his last nerve in hopes he would make a mistake I could take advantage of. I kept my eyes on his and kept on the pressure mentally hoping for something to distract him.

"You were pretty sly, Billy boy, planning so far ahead, but then a stupid mistake like hiring second raters to take me out in Marseilles and calling them from your yacht by cell."

He stared down at me with his head tilting like a dog who heard an odd sound. "Marseilles?" Then I saw the light in his eyes change. "Bitch!" He spat. I saw his eyes narrow and I knew he was going to squeeze the trigger.

I prepared to move, regardless of the chances when suddenly something at the door drew his eyes and he started to raise the gun to point it at the movement.

It was Mom dressed in a grey stealth suit and holding a bow.

I moved, rising up and snapping the gun out of his hand as I attacked him.

I automatically went to my father's style, *Sulsa do*, the way the Old Hwarang did it—using *Wae Gong* techniques of flesh ripping and drove three punches almost faster than the eye could follow into his chest. Fist to crack the ribs, bent fingers to push through the skin and a spear-hand straight fingered to drive into the chest cavity.

I did to him literally what he had done to me metaphorically. My father had done it once to a 300-pound pig as a demonstration to impress villagers in China during the war. The pig I was killing was not so impressive.

Carter had caused Dae Hoon's death and taken the love of my life from me so now I tore his heart from his body in a spray of blood.

I sank to the floor with all my energy spent as his body spasmed beside me.

My mother stepped up to me and put a hand on my shoulder.

"It's not over yet, *Haha*," I whispered.

"I know," she said. "But for now let us set the explosives to this place and go home; Banzai misses us."

Chapter Thirty-Three
FINGERED...

There was a lot of fallout from the affair at Liebfreid's Lair but we were able to make it look like a Russian mob attack on Count Vertigan. The Agency was pissed at me, but we were able to placate them with all the information that Emily had amassed on the financial empire that Carter had set up. I am pretty sure they were able to take over some of it and that always made the money-hungry agency very happy.

Then there was the healing, both physical and mental I had to do; to get my head straight and really think about what Carter had said. His last words *"Marseilles?"* then *"Bitch!"* had set me on another path and so I found myself in beautiful ancient Kyoto, ten months after Maria Carter's funeral, three months after I watched William Carter die in front of me.

I entered a teashop across from the *Ryoan-ji* temple rock garden where *she* was seated at a table, alone.

From a distance she looked no different from the hundreds of glossy black-haired women on the street, her raven hair cut into a sort of Dorothy Hamill retro cut.

She wore a simple, sleeveless dress with a light green pattern on it that suggested the ocean. Her only jewelry was a small gold bracelet on her left wrist, just above her four-fingered hand.

"Konnichiwa, Maria-sama," I slipped into the chair opposite her. Her dark eyes went wide—well, as wide as the eye surgery she'd had to try to pass for at least half-Asian would allow.

"Jon!" she was so shocked she didn't even try to bluff me out with an 'excuse me?' or 'you must be mistaken'. Instead she just asked, "How did you find me?"

"Find you? That was easy, once I thought to even look. I have a lot of relatives on this island, on both sides of the law. A nine-fingered woman, *Gaijan* or otherwise, gets noticed if you ask enough people."

"I had planned to have something done about that. I can't wear gloves all year round," she held up the pinkie-less left hand to consider it. "I just haven't found the right plastic surgeon."

"I am assuming you had the eye surgery done out of country?"

"Brazil," she sipped some tea with a nonchalance that was staggering. "But I was not completely happy with his work, so I decided to find someone else for the prosthetic finger."

We sat silently for a moment, the sounds of the city around us somehow receding so it felt as if we were in our own little bubble.

As I looked into her eyes, that were familiar and strange at once. Any feeling I had once had for her was trumped by the coldness I saw there when she asked, "How did you think to look?"

"I didn't at first," I said as frigidly as I could. "I actually cried for you, I really did. First time in a long time I'd done that. Then when I found William because of that careless phone call to second-rate thugs in Marseilles it all seemed too neat. When he seemed surprised about me even being in France it triggered a lot of things." She sipped her tea as if I was describing a recipe and I was astounded I had not seen this side of her before.

"Then things began to bother my sense of order. Other things were just too neat. Little things at first but there were so many of them. First the lousy driver trying to hit you at exactly the time I was on the street. Then when Dae Hoon was murdered, no one could have snuck up on him if he was not distracted or disabled. Or unless it was the very person he was leading to the hideaway spot; you! Why?"

"Why? I had to have you at a fever pitch to believe me, off balance and susceptible to my charms; there was no way to know you were so close when I sent his emergency alarm after he was dead. You were never supposed to meet any of those guys; it would have all been for nothing if they had killed you then. As it was, I had to radio the guys downstairs to leave. You cost the gang some very good operatives."

"I'll take pride in that."

She smiled. "That can't be all."

"Then there were those three clowns who attacked us in the woods. With billy clubs? Not tasers or guns. Nice to think you were sure I could beat their asses."

"Until that idiot Hiro pulled a gun," she said with disgust.

"You covered that up pretty well. Nice acting."

"Thank you."

"And again the same two with knives was a nice vote of confidence in me."

"Don't feel too complimented. I knew you had your gun."

"Noted." I said without humor. "Lastly the goons you called to attack me in Marseilles were just too low level; after I thought about them it was clear it was intended to be the breadcrumbs that led me back to William. You had to double cross him too; you are, like he said, a cold bitch. The maze you had in The Lair did delay me just enough for you and your too-trusting husband to make it to the preset conflagration at the boat house. Again, your confidence that I would find the traps is edifying."

The corners of the mouth I'd once thought pretty curled into a sly smile. "It should have been a perfect plan. How did you trick to that part?"

"It *was* almost perfect," I concurred. "Using your dead sister's ashes where enough of her teeth survived for a DNA read. Mixing in some of your toenails and hair to make the autopsy read like you were the body. It was just your decision to 'seal the deal' with your left pinkie finger that I realized later was overkill."

I let myself show a humorless smile.

"I mean, with all the yakuza connections in this it seemed to be too coincidental. The yakuza's habit of cutting off their little finger to make amends for transgressions came to mind. And once I thought of that I thought about your high threshold of pain and that was one coincidence too many. My family doesn't really believe in coincidence in these things."

"Maybe I should have given you a different finger." She gave a little laugh. "William and I planned to 'die' and disappear since before his wreck; he had already started looting the stock portfolios back then. He had started stealing from the Kobe Yamaguchi-gumi as well and that we couldn't have, so I planned to make it right with them after I got rid of him. Mind you, his accident was not as serious as he played it, but it suggested the final out we ended up planning and allowed him to get the plastic surgery ahead of time."

"It really almost did work, you know. And at first we were fooled by what they found of Carter as well."

"Yes," she confided. "We thought it would be enough to satisfy investigators. I wasn't so sure."

"Why did you two split up?"

"I decided I'd leave him as well as start a new life, though he thought we'd meet in six months 'casually' in Monaco…me an Asian and he, also changed with an Andorran passport. I didn't actually visit him in Stuttgart, by the way…just made the call from the river side so it would register with the same cell tower." She gave a little, proud of herself smile.

"And, actually, my finger was a little improvisation on the spot; I wanted to be very sure." She gave her cold laugh again and it sent a chill up my spine to think how her laugh used to thrill me. "He was a fool. I mean after the accident, any feeling I had for him died then. And why be tied to one man ever again when, as a rich Japanese-American widow I could have my pick. For all his ability to 'see the big picture' my darling husband couldn't see what was right in front of his nose. I figured when you caught up with him you would stop. I am betting you never gave him a chance to explain anything; you can be such a hothead."

"And because of that I was the perfect patsy,' I said bitterly. "An expert witness…but too blinded by renewed love for you to think too hard or too deep."

"You were supposed to be, Jon, but you're too much your father's son. Too suspicious."

"I get all my suspiciousness from my mom. She really never liked you, you know?"

We sat then for a time in silence, looking into each other's eyes, seeing what had been and what could have been.

"What now?" she asked. "I suppose the fact that I am filthy rich won't mean much to you?"

"You tried to kill my mom to 'throw me off' and you did kill Sammo. I could forgive you destroying me a second time, but you deliberately set up my cousin and murdered him. I will see you suffer for that."

Suddenly she had a small revolver in her hand that she pointed at me from the tabletop. She was farther across than I could jump quickly and I had my knees deep enough under the table I couldn't throw myself backward fast enough to avoid a shot. I kept my facial expression neutral.

"That the gun you used on Dae Hoon?"

"Yes, so you know it will do the job."

"The police are over there by the garden in plain clothes," I said, my voice flat. "They did me the courtesy of letting me have this conversation before they make the arrest. Murder, conspiracy, international fraud…not to mention illegal entry to Japan. Surrender now and they will take you into custody. You'll serve your sentence here; they won't extradite you to the U. S. unless the death penalty is taken off the table."

"No, Jon," she said with a smile that I would have once thought alluring. "I don't think so. No prison for me; I look terrible in orange."

Before I could act she turned the revolver and shoved it into her mouth. She locked eyes with me and in that last second, her steely demeanor fell away and I saw fear and maybe the long ago innocence I had once loved. Then she pulled the trigger and blew the top of her head off.

I sat there unmoving as her still beautiful face lost all the spark of life and fell forward to smash into the teacup and saucer with a crash.

There was a long moment of limbo when I saw images of her from twenty years ago superimposed over her in the motel room. Her smile, her eyes, glowing with love—or so I thought. There had been a big hole in my heart for so long that I thought would never be filled and now, that hole was hardened at the edges.

That time I didn't cry for her; my Maria had died a long time before.

The worse part of the whole thing would be listening to my mother say, 'I told you so' and knowing she was right; I do have terrible judgment with women.

THE END

ABOUT OUR CREATORS

AUTHOR

Teel James Glenn has stories have been printed in magazines from Weird Tales, Spinetingler, SciFan, Mad, Black Belt, Fantasy Tales, Pulp Empire, Sherlock Holmes Mystery, SciFan, Sixgun Western, Crimson Streets, Silver Blade Quarterly, Tales of Old, Blazing Adventures and scores of other publications and dozens of books and anthologies in many genres. His short story "The Clockwork Nutcracker" won best steampunk story for 2013 from Preditor and Editors poll.

He is also the winner of the 2012 Pulp Ark Award for Best Author, his website is: TheUrbanSwasbuckler.com

INTERIOR ILLUSTRATOR

Tedd Lehman - Grew up in rural Wisconsin. While he enjoyed drawing growing up, he didn't see a future in it. After getting a music recording degree from University Wisconsin Oshkosh, he was rhythm guitar in Reflesent Tide for a few years. He enjoys collecting comics during this time, and has been honing his artistic skills. You can see his work on the cover of "Doorkickers: Panzer demon ", and the waist gunner print with "Flying Fortress Remastered".

COVER ARTTIST

Rob Davis—began his professional art career doing illustrations for role-playing games in the late 1980s. Not long after he began lettering and inking, then penciling comics for a number of small black and white comics publishers- most notably for Eternity Comics, which eventually became Malibu Comics in the 1990s, on their book SCIMIDAR with writer R.A. Jones. Expanding his career he eventually began working at both DC and Marvel on likeness intensive comics like adaptations from TV shows like QUANTUM LEAP and STAR TREK's many incarnations. Primarily he worked on the DEEP SPACE NINE comics for Malibu. At Marvel he worked on the comics adaptation of Saturday morning cartoon PIRATES OF DARK WATER. After the comics industry implosion in the late 1990's Rob picked up work on video games, advertising illustration and T-shirt design as well as some small press comics like ROBYN OF SHERWOOD for Caliber.

Rob continues to do the occasional self-published comic book as well as publisher and designer for his small-press production REDBUD STUDIO COMICS. Rob is Art Director, Designer and Illustrator for the New Pulp production partnership AIRSHIP 27 collaborating with writer/editor Ron Fortier. Rob is the recipient of the PULP FACTORY AWARD for "Best Interior Illustrations" in 2010 and 2016 for his work on SHERLOCK HOLMES: CONSULTING DETECTIVE and has been nominated for the same award a number of times since. A collection of selected Rob's illustrations from Airship 27 has been published as PULP: THE ART OF ROB DAVIS available at Amazon.com and Barnes & Noble online with a second collection in the planning stages. He works and lives in Missouri with his wife and two children.

NIGHTMARE COUP

America's greatest fear is realized when **President Trent's personal helicopter, Marine One,** blows up with him aboard. At the same time, across the Atlantic, Air Force Two carrying Vice-President Duncan McNeil explodes while landing at Rome's international airport. Within hours a Palestinian radical fringe group called Vengeance claims credit for the assassinations. A shaken Speaker of the House, Oliver Holstein, is immediately sworn in as the new President.

Every intelligence agency of the free world is tasked with finding Husam al Din, the mysterious mastermind behind Vengeance. Then Italian officials report that the Vice-President's personal Secret Service agent miraculously survived the crash and is recuperating in a Roman hospital. What does he know? Can he provide intelligence that might uncover the inside agents responsible for the twin terror attacks? More importantly, is he still a target of Vengeance?

The stakes have never been higher as a cunning, ruthless foe prepares to unleash a nuclear holocaust on America's allies in the final Executive Gambit.

WAYNE CAREY

Executive gambit

AN AIRSHIP 27 PRODUCTION

PULP FICTION FOR A NEW GENERATION!

AIRSHIP27HANGAR.COM

NEW **PULP**

www.ingramcontent.com/pod-product-compliance
Lightning Source LLC
Chambersburg PA
CBHW050659290626
47170CB00015B/2090